Carrie Tiffany was born in West Yorkshire and grew up in Western Australia. She spent her early twenties working as a park ranger in Central Australia. Her first novel, *Everyman's Rules for Scientific Living* (2005), was shortlisted for the Orange Prize, the Miles Franklin Literary Award, the Guardian First Book Award and the Commonwealth Writers' Prize, and won the Dobbie Award and the WA Premier's Award for Fiction. *Mateship with Birds* (2011) was also shortlisted for many awards, and won the inaugural Stella Prize and the Christina Stead Prize for Fiction in the NSW Premier's Literary Awards. She lives and works in Melbourne.

CARRIE TIFFANY
EXPLODED VIEW

TEXT PUBLISHING MELBOURNE AUSTRALIA

textpublishing.com.au

The Text Publishing Company
Swann House
22 William Street
Melbourne Victoria 3000
Australia

First published by The Text Publishing Company, 2019
This edition published 2020
Reprinted 2020

Cover design by Chong W.H.
Page design by Jessica Horrocks
Typeset by J&M Typesetting

Printed and bound in Australia by Griffin Press, part of Ovato, an accredited ISO/NZS 14001:2004 Environmental Management System printer

ISBN: 9781922268662 (paperback)
ISBN: 9781925774221 (ebook)

A catalogue record for this book is available from the National Library of Australia.

This book is printed on paper certified against the Forest Stewardship Council® Standards. Griffin Press holds FSC chain-of-custody certification SGS-COC-005088. FSC promotes environmentally responsible, socially beneficial and economically viable management of the world's forests.

This project has been assisted by the Australian Government through the Australia Council, its arts funding and advisory body.

CONTENTS

Downhill and without resistance a car can lose adhesion and break free from the road. Roads have been prepared ahead of time to link known attractions, to improve desired routes.

But what if the car made the road? What if the tar spewed out warm and black in front of it?

Leave the house, start the engine, move off the gravel onto the fresh, hard crust. This road is fine. Be like this road, a dark rope reaching out to take you somewhere new.

MY FAMILY

Morning. Here is father man off to the office. He leaves the house. He laces his boots on the back step and walks across the lawn. He walks through the pine trees to the workshop at the corner of the block and rolls up the roller door. All of his tools are resting on the shadow board. All of the parts are there, filleted out on the bench in front of him.

Here is a bonnet propped open. Dirty hands father man has under the metal lid, dirty hands pecking. Check the terminal connections at the battery for tightness and freedom from corrosion. Check the battery in its carrier for looseness. The electrolyte in each cell must be topped up with special laundry water that a mother uses in her iron.

Father man spends his days at the bench or in the pit or under the bonnet. He checks, finds the fault, adjusts.

Nothing soft, nothing that bends, nothing that holds liquid, nothing that flows or splashes can be relied upon, in an engine. Over time a seal will always leak. The water will spill and be used up. There isn't much that's female in an engine. Oils and rubbers, acids and waters – these are the first places to look for faults.

Babette, our cat, likes to lie down in a patch of sun on the concrete ramp that leads into father man's workshop. She'll roll onto her back and lick the tufty fur on her stomach as if she's doing housework. Babette isn't from now – she belongs to the time before. Father man doesn't chase her away. He pretends that she doesn't exist.

Mother is at the bus stop down on the highway waiting to catch the 14 to town where she has a desk in an office with a drawer for her red handbag and her folding umbrella and her Cup-a-Soup. At lunchtime she can do word puzzles or read her Mills & Boon while she drinks the tomato soup from her Cup-a-Soup cup.

The football slaps into my brother's hands as he walks up the road to meet the bus to school. Sport is work for boys. Every day my brother must practise for the running bounce. There's nobody to make you get on the bus. My brother knows I am behind him on the walk up the road but once the bus door opens he doesn't look back.

You can keep walking. Walk the firewood tracks. Lie down on the C. Y. O'Connor pipeline. Walk to the tip and search the heaps. Climb the rubbish hill to watch the trucks on the highway gather speed, watch their cargo wobble as they take the corner, as they skirt the arrester bed. Then you can walk home and slip back in through the front window of your own house, or another house nearby. You can tiptoe around all day or go out into the garden and climb a tree. There's no need to speak. I talk to the skinks, but not to people. You have to stop listening to yourself to be able to speak. Seventeen days then, without speech. You are only lost to others – not inside yourself.

A little later. The sun is getting higher, but it doesn't touch me up here in the tree. The sunrays hit the bottom pane of frosty glass on the front door of the fat lady's house next door and then the middle pane. Once they hit the top pane the door opens and the fat lady appears as if she's been flushed out, as if she's surrendered. She closes the door and turns to lock it behind her, the key glinting back at the sun as she slips it from the tumbler. She comes out from under the porch, the sun shining through her curls, her scalp a boiled egg beneath them. Can she feel the halo? The virgin has a halo in the pamphlets the Mormons leave on the bus. The Mormon virgin is thin and clean with long yellow hair and a golden headband powered by sunlight. The fat lady next door has a frill of dirty sheepskin around her slippered feet and a stretchy purple dress that's hitched up at the front. The orange gravel receives one fat foot and then the other; the same pieces of gravel are moved around each day. She can't see me up here, high in the tree. But even if she could, even if she threw something, it wouldn't reach. The fat lady holds on to the hot air for balance. She pants as she reaches the letterbox. Her tongue is short and pointed like a trowel but it comes out just far enough to lick her fat lips. She pats the top of the red letterbox and I can hear, a little muffled through the leaves of the orange tree, the sound of the key in her hand making contact with the metal.

When I was small I thought that a letterbox was a miniature version of the house it fronted. Not cute like a doll's house, but real. I thought that inside the letterbox were the rooms, the furniture, the family, of the house behind it. I thought that you could test things there – going into a forbidden room, touching a dangerous item, speaking a word – and because the letterbox was small everything that happened in it could be measured and contained. I'm not embarrassed about this. Children are small. They have small thoughts; small items feel safe to them.

The fat lady has put so much meat around herself it has gone hard. Her sister too. When the fat lady next door meets the sister off the bus and they put their fat arms around each other on the driveway it's like two rocks are being cosy. The day the fat lady next door decided that she wanted to be hard and started to eat, did she tell her sister? Or did the sister just know, and then sitting in her own house that must be somewhere on the bus route, but I've never seen it, she started to eat so they could harden up together? They've been like this for as long as I can remember so I don't know if one of them got there first. Fat isn't like wadding or stuffing. When skin is stretched over fat it can still detect heat or cold. Skin always knows the difference between stroking and gouging.

It's hard to think that a man had a part in making the sisters. A man became a father to make them, and now they have gotten so hard they are no use to other men.

The fat lady's letterbox is empty. It is not the day for envelopes from the council or reminders from the podiatrist. It is not a day when I have written her name on an envelope and licked it shut with nothing inside. The hinge on the lid of the letterbox yawns as she closes it. The fat lady has nothing to hold in her fat hands. She puts them in the pockets of her purple dress, then she makes for the backyard to let the chickens out of their coop and sit farting on her deckchair among them.

∧

I climb down from the tree and walk along the road towards the fence on the far side of the fat lady's house. It's a brick house with matching eye-windows on its front face. There are three wires to slip through and the weeds and the gravel to cross on the approach to the rear wall of the laundry. The bricks stop at waist height; above them are trays and trays of dirty louvred glass. It's the same as pulling sheets of paper from an envelope, except the glass must be laid gently, in order, on the ground. Each louvre must be returned to its correct tray before leaving. Cobwebs will be torn and the glass will be smeary from my fingers, but the fat lady won't notice. Now the fat has come up she has gone inside herself. She has given up on looking.

The laundry has halfway air and halfway things that live outside and in: a tub splattered with lilac paint, dead tomato plants, gardening tools, a broken plastic laundry basket, bags of hen pellets, a greasy leather dog-collar hung on a nail. I know the tired sound of the doors. I know the dimness of the hallway, the dust on the lounge-room curtains that has matted together so it hangs proud of the lace now, in its own furry layer. The tick tick of the electric clock on the kitchen wall bounces through the serving hatch. When I was small I climbed up into that hatch and pulled the doors around me and sat waiting for the ticks to float over my head from the kitchen to the front room, kissing each one on its way through.

I kneel on the brown carpet in front of the fat lady's china cabinet. I like to run my tongue or my fingers over the lip of a lock. I don't want the old dishes inside the cabinet but I do want the key. I've searched the fat lady's house many times for the key. I'll know it as soon as I put it in my mouth and feel its bitings.

In olden times when girls were yellow with curly tresses and green velvet gowns they wore an iron clamp like a stirrup between their legs with a lock in the front. A charity belt? The boy from the petrol station could take it off me, but he'd need the key. Welding is at the end of the apprenticeship. The boy could steal the welding mask and wear it so I wouldn't have to look at his face as he put the key into the lock. How do you say to the fat lady, *I love you?* Which parts do you love – the older her underneath or what she's put on top? Her face is still pretty, I think. Her lips could still kiss.

The fat lady has left the margarine out on the kitchen bench so I put it back in the fridge. She keeps the tins in there too with the labels peeling off from the damp. There's nothing good for me to eat. The toaster is on the floor next to the rubbish bin. I shake the crumbs into the sink, plug it in and push the lever down; the array is dead again. The fat lady makes the same mistake as my mother: she uses a fork to release bread that's stuck in the grabbers, which snaps the nickel-chromium wires. In any machine the smallest part is often where the break occurs. I take the toaster's shell off with a butterknife, leaning over the bench so the screws fall in sight. The break in the wire is clean and there's enough slack to twist the broken ends together and re-establish contact. I test-toast two slices of white Tip Top and leave them there, peeking out of the bread grabbers, just lightly browned.

When I was small the fat lady didn't lock her house, not that I would have used the door. I know I have grown because now, when I come and go, I must remove and replace four rows of glass louvres. It was only three before.

I walk home along the road. The centre line, not near the verge. A road is a line of communication between houses. Everyone has a right to use it. It doesn't feel my feet on its flinty back. The road is mute; it cannot share what it knows.

And don't think that it was cruelty – putting the empty envelopes in the fat lady's letterbox. It was an experiment about hope.

My brother has sports practice after school so I work on the cars in the afternoons. Father man doesn't have a sign or a certificate. Word of mouth and cash in hand. It's always nice to lift a bonnet for the first time, like opening a suitcase to see the chosen items and admire how they've been packed. It's always nice to switch a new engine on and watch the parts clicking and turning over each other – leads sprouting from the plugs, the head squat and centred like a roast in its tray.

Collect chocks and place within easy reach. Loosen upper suspension fulcrum shaft bolt and chock the arm suitably to hold it in its uppermost position. Empty the sump; bleed the lines. Check batteries and fuses. I have a kerosene drum and a toothbrush to clean the parts. A strip-down is an operation. Douse the part, brush it, rinse it and replace it on the tarpaulin, each part winking in its blue puddle under the sun. A doctor has his nurse to count the parts in and out. I have my two girl's hands. Here I am running my fingertips around each screw and bolt, making a sieve with my fingers to scoop out the fat flies that come down to drink.

It's best to stay outside the workshop. In the summer the tops of the trees are tinselled by the sun. You can wash a car out here and give it back without a service; they always say it runs better. I do tyres too. It isn't easy to get a tyre off a wheel but I don't complain. The Holden badge is a lion with its paw on a round rock. When cavemen saw lions rolling rocks with their paws they must have been happy to know the wheel was discovered. It still looks hard, the wheel, hidden inside the dark rubber tyre; the cavemen would still recognise it. But the cab, the chassis, the armature, the weight of all the car's parts, sits on air. The real invention was not the rolling of the rock, but the trapping of the sky around it – making a rubber cushion covering for the air. When the surface of a tyre rips, you can see the rubber is woven together like blankets. There are tyre irons with rounded edges to lever the beads off the tyre, one at a time, from the inner flange of each wheel. The inner tube is flaccid, a flop of grey tongue. You drown it in a bucket. You hold it under so bubbles escape through the hole and it tells you where it is cut.

In the winter, rain drips through the trees. The mating surfaces of the ball joint stud and the knuckle tapers must be clean and dry. You do everything forwards and then you do it in reverse. A frog opens its throat in the grass. When it rains you can sit for a while in father man's blue Holden, or in a repair. When father man is out you can slide behind the steering wheel. Ignition. Foot pressed to metal plate. And again. Petrol surges through the lines. The sweet smell of it firing. Tightnesses. The way one part greets and enters another.

There's a blanket on the back seat of father man's Holden. It's a checked picnic blanket that my mother has put there. It's from the time before. It's easy to see that plastic novelty items like yo-yos won't be around in the future. They are cheaply made – they are just for the moment. But a blanket made of wool will give warmth forever. The label says *Household Linens Pty Ltd* and the corner of it has been snipped off with a pair of scissors, which I think means there was something imperfect about it. That it was going cheap.

When the work is done I go back to the house to make margarine jam toast for my brother and pretend to do my homework. My brother is one year older but not much taller than me. We watch *Hogan's Heroes* together. I pick Louis the Frenchman. All the girls want the American in the leather cap, but he knows it and you can see his hair is wearing off. In the last credits before *Matlock Police* we get the ice cream out of the freezer and put it on top of the television. My brother moves it around with a golf putter so it cools all of the wood on top of the television and he doesn't have to get up off the couch. Sometimes when our mother gets home from work she puts her hand there, near the rabbit's ears, to see if it is hot, and she'll tell father man about it because we were using electricity that they had bought together, that wasn't free, that didn't belong to us, that didn't grow on trees.

My mother gets home from work and there is no food in the fridge for dinner. She takes the Holden to go shopping. It's just the two of us. It's what girls and women do.

A car settles into a corner. A bench seat is good for

settling a child. Father man has settled on my mother. The man with the swollen neck who packs bags in the supermarket might settle on me.

The man collects the trolleys from the supermarket car park when it is so hot it burns to touch the metal of them. His hair and skin are red. He wears thick glasses with plastic frames. I don't know how he can be inside himself with that sharp vinegar sweat on his skin and in his clothes. Nobody talks to him. It's best to keep your eyes down when he's packing the shopping. Today, when he has a tin of peas in his hand, when soft things, bananas and bread, are building up around him but he is saving them for the tops of the bags, he says that my hair is nice.

The cash register pings and rests and pings again. He wasn't to know that I don't speak. That bit wasn't his fault. I flick my eyes over his face as we leave. His chin is stained with blue pen. Just a second to rub that off, if he'd had someone to tell him it was there.

On the way home my mother stops at the petrol station. I don't get out of the car. I don't want the boy from the petrol station to see me with my mother. I look into the side mirror so I can see everything that's happening behind. Here we are pulling away from the bowser, the road rushing away in retreat. Dead grass on the nature strip. A bus shrinking, fading, as it gears down to take the hill. Everything shuddering as the tyres burr and slap the road.

Backwardness. More backwardness. Everything spooling out, collecting behind us. The reflected view is pitted along the bottom edge where the side mirror's surface has worn away and the black paint underneath shows through. Fences made from roofing iron. A covered trailer parked, for sale. A sign for the new Olympic swimming pool, and then the long, gravel-packed cage of the truck arrester bed. The view inverts, retreats, rushes to be gone from.

Across, in the driver's seat, my mother in profile, her neck severed by a gold jewellery chain like she is on the face of a coin. She watches the bitumen ahead. She joggles the wheel from side to side although the road is straight. She doesn't look in the mirror.

I wind my window down, let the warm insect air hit my face. The view behind us is long now, so long it loops back on itself like the toffee they stretch in the caravans at the royal show. The weight of it? If there is so much view behind us will it be heavy? Will it drag us back? A sweet spot on the road, and for a second the car is quiet. The view, just then, sharpens into focus but nothing much is being reflected – just a pile of old gravel heaped next to the road and the grey forest still and hot behind it. The car is connected to the retreating view only through my eye. I can't look away, not until we turn off the main road, curve into the driveway and park under the pine trees, the engine cut but tick, tick, ticking with heat.

Things are mostly brown here, where we live. My mother, my brother, father man and me. The gravel, the paint on the house, the rust along the bottom of the car door. I am brown-haired. There's only so much yellow hair to go around and people miss out. If you are yellow you have a yellow name like Jodie or Denise and you have to wear shorts. If everyone was yellow it wouldn't be so special and men would take another colour and make it the best for themselves. My mother started out brown. She was brown in the time before. There is a photograph of my mother holding a baby in a laundry basket on her hip. My brother is a plump grub in with the sheets and towels. My mother has messy brown hair and a floaty blouse and beads on a leather cord at her throat. A grown-up woman can make herself new for the man that wants to settle on her. For father man my mother has yellow hair that's combed straight, each strand its own thin, separate rope.

At home now, the car must be gotten out of. The brown house must be approached and entered. The view can't be shattered. It always brings us back to here. You can't go straight to your room. You have to bring in the shopping bags and touch them and open the fridge as if you are putting something in or taking something out. You have to take the cat food out to the laundry. Everybody in a family, even when it has made itself ugly, has to help.

I have something special in my room. Something I want to get back to. Hidden under the bed is the manual for father man's blue car. *Scientific Publications Holden Workshop Manual Series No. 51*, in its protective plastic cover, with its rub of grease across the front.

If you had never touched an engine, if it were only a matter of looking in the manual, you would think it was a miracle, that it couldn't have been made by a man. The front wheel hub and drum assembly – hub bolt, grease-retaining seal, inner bearing, drum attaching bolt, outer bearing, castellated nut – all gilded, all snug up, side by side. Perfect, glossy, tight. When the creamy paper rears up at me I can see how the parts fit together. I can see the exploded view.

In the manual you can choose to look at the parts, or the air in between them. The air in between isn't nothing; it isn't blank. If you make yourself look for what's not there the empty spaces become parts themselves. The empty spaces become air parts, bordered by the metal and rubber. In *Exploded View of Water Pump Assembly* the air part around the fan looks like a design for a jigsaw puzzle of a windmill. Steerarma, hubner, suspenister. Why not? Why shouldn't the air parts have a name? If you cast only the air parts in steel and assembled them the engine would be peaceful, then. It would be beautiful. The engine would be made from air.

The place where a part connects is specially prepared with a housing, a rim, a thread or a flange. One true surface against another. It's not possible for the parts of the body to fit together like this. There's skin and there's the flesh under it. The flesh, the meat of the body, isn't stable. There are three lines cut into the leather of father man's belt. The deepest cut is in the middle to fit his regular girth, then there's a shallower cut next to the hole on either side for thinner days and fatter days.

Probably every manual or every book exists within another book, and every picture probably exists within another picture if you could just use your eye to cut it up and reassemble it to make the pieces anew. Each new thing is just a version of something else. It's the order that changes – perhaps you can save yourself by putting things in a different order? My mother, myself. It means you are part of something but it also means that you can't get free.

It is safe in my room after dinner and I lie on the bed. A juvenile skink comes in through the hole in the flyscreen and slides down the wall beneath the window. The skink's toe suckers work for rocks and bark, but not so much on paint. If you are a skink you only have two speeds: still and rushing. A skink never moseys along.

Once, when I skipped the bus, I challenged myself to walk as slowly as I could to the tip to get time over with.

That's what school is useful for – getting through time. I didn't stick at the slowness. Perhaps I am a person that doesn't stick at anything? The colonel on *Hogan's Heroes* says you can let life happen to you, or you can go out and take it by the horns. The colonel doesn't have trouble taking the girls in their white frilly blouses and taking stolen goods out of trucks and taking the mickey out of Colonel Klink. Life is always easier for Americans.

The skink that came through the window into my room wants to get out again. It can make it over the skirting board and up the wall, one foot, two foot, towards the window, then its toes lose stickiness and it falls. After six attempts it stops being good to watch. The skink can't turn in the air like a cat does to make sure it lands on its feet. It falls flat and stupid like a piece of toast with its margarine side down. Soon it will break apart, then Babette will eat it. I wait until the skink has clambered up a foot or so, then I put the Holden manual underneath it, perpendicular to the wall, and use it gently, like the rising floor of a lift, to boost the skink up to the window and then safely out. I'm not saying this because it seems kind, only because it was useful.

It's nice to imagine the skink opening its gummy mouth and telling its family about its adventures in its squeaky skink voice. The human voice is made in a box in the throat. When there's damage or a fault you get an electrical voice that sounds like a robot to hold under your chin. There's a lot you can do with your head and your neck and your shoulders to take the place of speech. If your mother asks you to get her a glass of water while she's watching television you fetch it. *Did you feed the cat?* Nod, half-nod, partial shrug, slow blink, faster blinks, shoulder jerk. Perhaps I have invented another language? Nearly thirty days now. A seal forming in the throat. A hard layer settling across the box of the voice.

Last thing at night, before he goes to bed, father man unclips the key chain from the belt loop of his shorts and does the locking up. Father man has the key to the outside lock that keeps us out, and the inside lock that keeps us in. He doesn't have his outside boots on; he has brown rubber thongs on for inside the house. The soles of the rubber thongs stick to the lino and release a squelch with each footstep. Twice the key must go around to slide the bolt across, and in the morning twice again to bring it home. That's what a deadlock is — a tool that can't be roused or argued with. The deadlock protects us from danger. The deadlock doesn't know if the danger is on the outside or the inside. For a brief time, while he is walking the keys from the kitchen to the door and back again, father man holds us in his hand.

Once a Mormon came on a bicycle sliding through the gravel. He rode up the driveway, dismounted and leant his bicycle against the front of the house. It was lunchtime and all of this we could hear while holding our sandwiches up to our mouths. The Mormon knocked and knocked on the front door. It was hot. He might have liked a glass of water. The front door of the house has never been opened or unlocked. Father man said the sandwiches had been made and the sandwiches had to be eaten. Fresh food always has to be eaten when it is fresh. The Mormon kept on knocking. His knock grew weaker as we chewed, then sharp again with its last rap to tell us that he knew we were inside.

If the house caught fire at night we would be found with our faces pressed to the locked door as the flames licked at us, as the fire melted our hair. We would die before we went to father man's coat to touch the keys to the deadlock. Or perhaps we already have?

The window is my night-escape. I peel the flyscreen back from its frame and climb through. I like to walk on our road in the dark. Chips of iron in the bitumen. If father man pushes you down on the road in the summer the tar will stick. Grease on your wrists, stains on your clothes. No need to tell, he says. But tonight the road is clean and cool. The blackness gets right up against you, rests on your shoulders and your hips, gets in between the strands of your hair, curls into the space between the legs of your jeans. All your expressions are safe in the dark. It doesn't matter that you are having cruel thoughts and that your face is ugly while you are having them.

Later, back in my bed and waiting for sleep, I listen to the trucks braking on the highway. It means all the parts are working – the foot of the driver against the pedal, the hydraulic cylinder pushing the brake shoe, the lining of the brake shoe pressing the inner surface of the drum. Friction turning motion into heat. If a part is broken the heavy truck on the steep hill becomes a runaway. Any animal or person on the road can become its victim.

The arrester bed is a reassurance. A bed of gravel to control what is out of control. The driver of the runaway truck steers into the cage of the arrester bed. The gravel within the cage pushes between the wheels, seeps into the suspension, into the cavities around the engine, smothers the speed and its danger and brings the truck to a stop.

I imagine the soft body of the driver against the hard gravel as it floods into the cabin of the truck, a pillow of gravel collecting around his face. It must feel like being held; it must feel like an embrace.

A hot day, still. It's a Saturday and father man makes me lie down in the dirt to mark out the distance between the uprights for the new back fence. I am five feet tall. Father man says, 'no need to measure.' Five feet between each upright. The post-hole digger is like a shovel but it twists out a neat, round mouthful of dirt. The post-hole digger grips at my hair and drags it down into the mix. Father man doesn't tell me that I'm allowed to get up again, but I can hear when the post-hole digger is deeper than my skull. A firm impression has been made; it's all right to stand up now.

We don't live on soil. We live on stones. The post-hole digger loosens the stones and makes them separate. On the top layer the smallest stones are round and perfect like orange pottery peas. Somehow weak pale grass grows on top of this and flattens it out and makes where we live look like everywhere else. I shake the stones out of my hair. I walk over to the trailer, select a new post and roll it over so it will be ready for its hole. Building the fence only takes half a day and it looks nice when the wires have been fed through the holes in the uprights and the fence is finished. It looks like the land matters so much to someone it has been given a necklace to wear.

My mother watches the fence going up as she pegs the underpants on the washing line. Babette mews at my mother's ankles because she doesn't understand what's happening above her and it must seem like my mother is dancing. The adult male underpants and the adult female ones hang next to the boys' fourteen-plus and the girls' twelve-and-up. They are all mixed in together as they go from wet to dry and nobody says one word about that.

It was a shock to see the crop of black hair down there. When I was a child I thought the black hair was to hide a join between the legs and the body, a join that was needed when the new parts came in. I thought there was a clasp, or perhaps a ridged line like on a jam jar where the top screws down. I didn't think the black hair would happen on me. After it started to happen I couldn't look at a man with a tight black beard that covered his lips and made his mouth look like a hole. If I stood close to a man with a beard like that I thought people would know what was happening to me.

After lunch, when the fence is finished, Darren comes over to help father man remove the Holden's engine with a block and tackle attached to a beam under the workshop roof. Both Darren and father man think they alone are doing the heavy lifting, that the other man is not pulling his weight.

'Hold the cunt,' father man says as the engine sways above him. 'Hold the cunt still.'

The wooden rafter moans as the rope bites into it. Darren strains and rearranges his weight at the end of the rope.

'I am holding the cunt still,' he says, but his voice is soft like plastic.

With two men there is always the man that makes the words and the man that repeats them. It's not decided by age or size, but which of them is crueller, to others and to himself.

When they are finished with the hoist father man gives Darren a beer and they lean against the bonnet of Darren's white Valiant. Darren lights their cigarettes with a tiny match he rips from a cardboard matchbook. His forearms are covered in a sleeve of hair. Blue singlet. Black football shorts. Workboots. When sitting, one withered apricot ball pressed against his thigh.

Darren lives between the shire reserve and the tip and the new housing estate. He tells father man how he found a shire raincoat at the tip and that when he hears people cutting timber for firewood in the reserve he puts the shire raincoat on and hooks his trailer up and drives in to tell them that they need a permit. Then he tells them that he likes them, so he won't report them, but they should unload the wood from their trailer into his trailer. Darren sells the trailer-loads of firewood to the people who live on the new housing estate.

Father man and Darren crack another can and Darren says the thing is, lately, when he goes out to his car in the morning there's a human shit on it. First morning the shit is on the bonnet, right in the middle, next morning it's on the windscreen, and then on the roof and that can't have been easy because the roof is slippery and there's a roof rack. Yet the shit, Darren reckons, is large. Adult-sized, he says.

Father man whistles through his teeth and shakes his head as if he's trying to tip the shit, or the thought of the shit, out of his ear. They talk about the Valiant and what needs to be done to her, and then they talk about my mother.

Babette is tiptoeing around father man with her back arched, rubbing her sides against his legs. An animal doesn't know what shame is. An animal never feels tainted.

Darren goes home and in the afternoon the lady with the pink plastic glasses who lives on Struttle Road comes to pick up her Mazda. Father man tells her the best thing to do is to drive the Mazda into the ground. Every car is a collection of failures waiting for their time and place. When the failures are so great the car is no longer worth repairing.

Then Mrs Thomas drives up in her white Morris and she and the car are all tilted to the side. She sits side-saddle, with her knees together, a crocheted cushion under one buttock. Her pantyhosed feet reach out to operate the pedals as if she's playing the piano. A car will go where the driver looks. Mrs Thomas's head is sideways on her neck like a bird's. She scrapes fences, is a danger in the car park. On television, when the driver is speaking to the passenger – a man to his wife – he will look at her face but keep driving straight ahead so you know he's not really driving. There's something rigged up with the camera that you can't see. Mrs Thomas doesn't have a television set, or maybe it was in for repairs when I climbed through her toilet window and into her little white house.

The corner swells ahead. Father man is doing a test drive in Mrs Thomas's car. I am in the back seat, for later. There is a broken headlamp on the seat beside me. Father man returns the broken parts, sometimes on a rag if they are greasy, to prove that clean new parts have been installed in their place. It isn't always true. He doesn't buy new parts from the automotive supplier; he has no account. If a replacement part is essential he has his own carcasses stacked behind the workshop to harvest from, and in the town down the hill there are fields and fields of wounded cars in the pick-and-pay.

'Your receipt is in the back,' father man says, as a joke, when a customer hands over the cash. Especially with a female, any broken part will do. At her last service Mrs Thomas took home the burnt-out motor of our vacuum cleaner. She clucked her tongue and shook her head at it through the window of her Morris.

'So it was you,' she said to the tiny plastic motor, 'that caused all that trouble.'

The next day an Alfa comes in for brake pads. I don't like its crimson panels, its bumper bar like a crooked lip. The Alfa-man wears a cap with Alfa written on it and the Alfa badge with the snake and the cross. He says the car is a ground-up resto and that he only paid a finger for it. He says when it's finished it will be worth a hand.

It's a dark night. The spring-loaded bonnet of the Alfa comes up like the tongue of an envelope, bounces a little and then hits me in the head. The next night when I drive the Alfa down the hill a clutch of golf balls roll forwards under the pedals. When I drive it back up the hill they roll under the seat and wait in the rear again.

Stopped at the stop sign on the highway, I hear a telephone ringing sadly behind the door of a house. It is surprising how tight the steering wheel is, the resistance of it in your hands and arms. When I was a child I thought the wheel went all the way around, that there was no end to its turning. But really it is more like a shoulder – it is attached, in a complicated way, to the other working parts, none of which are any use at all if they are on their own.

I like that you have to look forwards, when driving,

to see what's coming up behind. The windscreen frames the view nicely. It favours the road, of course. You could look elsewhere, off to the dark hills, up to the stars in the sky, but the windscreen makes you keep the road in mind. Everything is set up for that.

Remember to return seats, side mirrors and the rear-vision mirror to their original positions after you have stolen the keys to a repair and driven it through the night.

I go to the tip the next day and come home when I'm hungry. After dinner my brother falls asleep on a slice of bread and father man uses the pincers. If the pincers were big enough it wouldn't have hurt. It could have looked pretty even – my brother's neck decorated with the shining pincer jaws.

My brother had been sentenced to the table with his plate of peas. He didn't know how to hide vegetables in the pockets of his cheeks. Next to the plate of peas was a bread-and-butter plate with a white slice. I'm not sure if my brother slumped suddenly onto the white slice or rested his cheek on it gently. His face was shut and the slackness in his feet under the table told me he wasn't foxing, he was really asleep on the slice of bread.

Father man saw my brother asleep on the bread through the kitchen window. He went to the workshop. He fetched the pincers from the shadow board. He took off his boots at the back door so as not to make a sound. He crept up behind my brother. Father man opened the pincers but they were too small. The shape they made was oval. My brother's neck is round. My brother's neck is a soft boy's neck; his man apple hasn't come up yet in the front.

Pincers are for working with nails and any sorts of metals that stick and pluck and pull. Crabs and scorpions can inject venom during a pincer strike. Father man hooked my brother up by the neck. The bread came with him, I think because his saliva was on it. The frame of the bread was stiff but the white within it was soggy. It made a hole, easily, for the cry to get through.

My mother rushed in. There was shrieking and the pincers were put in a drawer. Kitchen tools are called utensils, small tools suitable for women. The pincers lay next to the scissors, side by side, in the kitchen drawer.

Afterwards father man had his shower. He took his outside work socks off and put his inside rubber thongs on. He fetched the key and locked the locks.

Another option at night, if there's no sleep, is to lie in bed and do some engine breathing. Starting at rest, then the cough of first ignition. Cold early combustion, cloudiness in the chest as the oil stretches and heats. Once the motor is ticking smoothly I move up the gears and down again. The throat grasps the changes. The mattress is a soft road beneath the breathing engine. It allows the shudders of the motor to enter but it doesn't pass them on. Later in the night I put the engine under load – a hill at first, increasing in steepness, then a trailer, increasing in weight. In the dark there is a tug of war between the dead weight of the load and the power of the engine. There is no shame in losing. Any engine, any body, can be outmatched. It goes on until the breath is broken, my pillow is wet and the day birds start to sing.

The next day is a Sunday and it is hot again. People are coming outside and then not being able to decide if they want to be outside, so they go inside again. People are coming outside and then going inside again like dogs.

In the glove box of the Holden there is a photograph of father man. Something is wrong with father man's body. He is younger in the photograph. He is barely a full man yet. Here he is standing next to a pockmarked termite mound in a field of pockmarked termite mounds. The red dirt from the mound is smudged on his shorts and his t-shirt. The air around him is smudged and gingery too. There are his hands, hanging from his wrists, hanging from his arms, hanging from his shoulders. Have I ever seen father man without a tool in his hands? What did he believe in back then? There's a green can of course.

A perfect fit for the palm. Father man's thumb and fore-finger nearly meet, in a pincer grip, around the shiny green can.

When father man was a baby he was brought home from hospital on the bus. There was no car then and no shoes. There were cigarettes and a tractor for tending the paddocks around the fruit trees. Father man didn't say when he got prickles in his square boy's feet. He had some cut-down tools but he didn't have words or songs. His dad gave him a cigarette for his birthday. He might have been five. He might have been nine when the first car came but I imagine he always knew how to press his lips together wetly to make the sound of a motor, always knew how to hold his spittle to mimic the dead place in the gearbox between the gears. When his infant teeth rotted and ached father man drove himself to sleep. He knitted the car, the camber of the road, the cadences of the motor in a side pocket of his cheek that didn't hurt. He always put the tools back on the shadow board after he had used them.

The thing I really know is that father man dropped a hammer on his bare five-year-old foot. Three toes broke and the nails greyed and died. His mother heated a darning needle to pierce the nails and release the black blood behind them. Father man took the hot needle between his own boy's fingers and went out under the

42

fig tree and did it to himself. It's a choice to hurt yourself before someone else gets a chance.

If you decide to go to school, a Monday can be good. People might not remember that you weren't there on the Friday because they have been having happy times with their families on the weekend. On a Monday the teacher won't ask you a question because they're sunburnt from playing veterans' cricket and they always start the class by asking the boys about their kicks and hits and runs. Recess is just two laps of slow walking around the quadrangle. Lunch is twelve. When the bell goes for lining up you can take your place. You can be close to someone behind you and close to someone in front of you. They might not like it but there's punishment for talking so they can't say, and that's fine by me.

There are many happy times in my family. The happiest time is when my mother loses a contact lens. She calls us to her and we drop to our knees and pat the floor at her feet. It mainly happens in the bathroom, so she's wearing her slippers or her feet are bare on the brown tiles. She doesn't move for fear of stepping on the lens but she calls down instructions telling us where she thinks we should look. Once I found the lens on the leg of her bell-bottoms, just under her knee where the fabric skirts out. A tiny glass cup stuck to the blue denim. I picked it off and put it in my mouth.

The thing that happened at school last year was a teacher became in love with a year nine girl. After a while the girl got a boyfriend, a boy from her own class at school, so she told the teacher that she wasn't going around with him anymore. On the weekend the teacher took fourteen fishing hooks from his tackle box and swallowed them, and then he called the ambulance. He's back at school this year. The scar on his throat where they cut him open starts at the top button of his short-sleeved business shirt and goes downwards. The girl isn't at school now, but when it happened she was fourteen years old.

Some cars come back to the workshop because they are weak and have broken down. Some cars come back because father man has failed to help them, or in helping them he has accidentally caused another part to fail. Some cars come back because of me. Darren's white Valiant is towed up the driveway on its rear wheels by a tow truck. The car has an unhappy, shameful feeling – a dog being dragged home after running off. The tow truck driver hands father man a clipboard from the cab – there's something for him to sign – then the driver reverses the winch and the front of the Valiant is lowered to the ground. The big white car sits under the pine trees. The big white car brought to silence so easily. A handful of my mother's sewing needles dropped into the carburettor, through the damper cap.

Tonight my mother is reading *Tangled Shadows*. Before that it was *Sweet Compulsion*; before that it was *Lure of Eagles*. Each book takes three days. She writes the titles down in a notebook in her red handbag so she doesn't get the same book from the library and read it twice. My mother is reading *The Tempestuous Flame*, *The Vital Spark*, *The Joyous Adventure*, **Stranger on the Beach** and *A Very Special Man*. My mother is full of romance. She carries it with her wherever she goes.

Christmas is just around the corner now. What is fancy on Christmas Day is when you take a watermelon and cut it in half and scrape out all of the flesh with a spoon to make it into a bowl. Then you fill it up with other fruit – grapes, bits of oranges and apples, some plums and tinned peaches. There is ice cream or cream with that.

What is also fancy at Christmas time is to have decorations. All the fathers in Australia hang strings of coloured lights – sometimes blinking lights. The father checks all the tiny bulbs and untangles all the lines. He doesn't like doing it but he does it all the same. The lights go up every year before Christmas and come down again afterwards.

It's Saturday again and I'm going Christmas shopping. Do I tell the bus driver that the white smoke coming out of the exhaust of his bus is a symptom of head gasket failure? Do I tell him that a poorly sealing rocker cover gasket will piss oil all over his engine? It's the big-belly bus driver again. He looks like he's rolled a rock into place above his dick.

'Must remember to buy coffee,' I say under my breath as I walk down the aisle of the bus. I don't drink coffee but it's something I mumble to myself. I got it from TV.

Sharon gets on the bus at her stop down the hill. She sits next to me because we're not at school so nobody can see. Sharon tells me that the boy that did the petrol at the local petrol station is now a tyre-fitting apprentice at the automotive next door. The boy gets four dollars for each tyre so every day he can buy Fanta and smokes. I've seen that boy – he wears Amco jeans and a silver chain around his neck. The tyre black is blackest around his fingernails, then grey across his knuckles. The boy is really just a child. Sharon says she milks him on the spare parts bench. She doesn't let him touch her because the tyre black might come off on her and she has good clothes now that she got from her mother's new boyfriend for her birthday.

The bus stops on the highway opposite the automotive. Sharon stands up and slides the top window of the bus open and puts out her hand and waves at the roller door across the road. The tyre boy is sitting on a milk crate in the sun in his black jeans with his black fingers around a smoke. He holds the smoke in the male way with his fingers curved around the top of it as if he's putting a hose to his mouth to drink. Females hold the smoke between two fingertips so it looks like they're blowing a kiss when they drag. I've practised this with a twig so when the time comes I'll know how to do it right.

The boy's arms are still thin. The chain with the key has gone inside his singlet between his nipples where there isn't any hair. Sharon doesn't mind that he hasn't grown into a man yet. He doesn't look up when Sharon calls and waves. The boy is all there is and Sharon is fine about taking it.

Three seats in front of Sharon and me, a man and a woman are sitting on the bus together. The man reaches behind the woman and puts his hand under her hair and strokes the warm part at the back of the woman's neck. His hand is hidden beneath her hair but I know it is there. She isn't a girl. Her hair is old. I can see the backs of their heads and I can see the side of the man's face. His nostril is curved up so the veiny red skin inside his nose is on show. It's revolting, but perhaps the woman has gotten used to that? When people become adults they can get used to anything.

Everybody knows that they want to touch you at the start. They like to go swimming with you. They like it when you're wet. They like it when you laugh, but not so much they can see the inside of your mouth. Hair hanging down your back is good. What I don't know is how you make them keep wanting to touch you. It's the first time I've seen it. I want to ask the woman on the bus the thing she has that is special because it doesn't show. What I need is for someone to tell this to my mother.

Sharon has bubblegum but she doesn't offer it. Just before we get off the bus I hold a plastic bag in front of her so she can change into her mother's new t-shirt because it is pink and has a low v-neck.

At the pharmacy there's a plastic stand of eye shadows to steal and there's a pencil for drawing a line around your lips and eyes. It's the same idea as at primary school – a decorative border to draw attention. Even if you do bad work in English or social studies the teacher will give you extra marks for the border.

Females aren't born with the lines drawn in. The rim of the eyes, the edges of the lips – the soft openings for crying and spitting – have to be outlined with a special pencil. There's an everyday size and a mini for the purse. When a male sees the lines they keep him up close. They keep him focused on the wet places of the face so he doesn't notice the female's outer edges and can't tell if she is made badly, or too young or too fat. *Treat yourself with Revlon*. Do they mean like medicine, or like on your birthday when you are meant to get cake? After you've treated yourself and it's in your pocket or your schoolbag the stealing makes your thighs swell and fill the tubes of your jeans. Even if you walk out carefully, one denim thigh rubs roundly against the other. It's best to tie your spray jacket around your waist, even in the summer. If you get caught you can say you didn't do it. What you say will come out of your drawn-around mouth so they might not listen; they might just watch the edges of it and see how it moves.

I take a bottle of my mother's perfume from the pharmacy. Every mother should smell nice. My mother wears the same perfume as she did in the time before, but perhaps it doesn't matter. The ad for Tweed says it is a woman's finishing touch. The perfume bottle is opaque. It has no gauge. It isn't like a petrol tank. You don't know it's empty until you spray the last spray. Back at home I replace the old bottle of perfume with the new. I like to take care of my mother. I like her to have the things a woman has. I like to keep her safe.

No one is home when I get back and there's time in the afternoon to bury the old bottle of perfume under the lemon tree in the front garden. I dig a deep hole with a trowel. I scoop out the dry orange stones on the top and the moist orange stones underneath. I put the perfume bottle at the bottom of the hole and I put the pincers in too.

The first time father man came for dinner my mother toothpicked a circle of pineapple to the top of the ham steaks, each toothpick crowned with half a red cherry on its tip. My mother wore lipstick. She told father man all about her job and she didn't have her Mills & Boon open on the table.

Just the round slab of ham at dinnertime tonight. My mother's mouth opens. She closes it. Tomato sauce helps with getting meat down. It's sad when adults stop wanting sweet foods.

The cricket is on the television. In between overs father man asks me what I want for Christmas. He is cutting his ham steak into a grid of equal forkfuls. Father man flicks his eyes from the television to me. He asks me again what I want for Christmas. The hot room. The pink meat. A fly whining at the window. He asks me again what I want for Christmas, but this time he says *girl*.

My mother is looking at me. I can feel the hard corners of her smile. There are no words inside me. I couldn't make them if I wanted to. Father man puts his knife and fork down. He gets up from the table. He goes to the kitchen drawer and takes out the scissors. Father man's face is blazing. I can hear him counting under his breath. He stands behind me. He grips my ponytail hard in his hand. He cuts off my hair.

My mother's shrieking was a kind of language. If she had kept shrieking I think I could have worked out what she was saying; I think I could have joined in. We might have had a conversation. But she stopped. She used her hand to stroke her own hair back behind her ear, then she put the ponytail in the kitchen bin.

After dinner I go to bed and read the newspaper. Another death for Ford today. A tussle between a car and a truck on the highway. The truck ended up in the arrester bed, but not before it ran over the Ford. The death count is just for today. Tomorrow it will revert to zero.

The night is warm and still, good for driving. I peel back the flyscreen and climb out onto the verandah. Babette is curled up, asleep, on my brother's schoolbag. She doesn't look up. A few steps across the dry lawn, then the dead needles beneath the pine trees. There's a Falcon in for service but tonight I want to drive father man's car. The door is open, the key a lump under the rubber mat. A Holden is something to be proud of. Holden is a family business that started out making saddles for horses, then they made motorbikes, then great Australian cars.

I like driving in the dark. If father man looked at the gravel in the morning he would see where the tyres of the cars turned in the night. He would see their slithered tracks like fat snakes winding down the driveway. The cars are happy not to have their lights switched on. They like to use my eyes. The slope down the driveway is steep enough for a family sedan to start rolling but sometimes I have to put my leg out and push along the ground to get first traction. The front tyres hold their breath, then tip into a forward roll. I can feel the exact moment when the tyres decide to shoulder the weight. Close the door gently. Sit tall as the car glides past the dark house as if it is a room that has broken free and is sliding slyly away from the others. It's safe to start the motor on the road after the bus stop. Even on a still night the sound barely carries and who's to say, anyway, what car this is on the road, and who is driving it? It's safe to drive up the driveway on the way home as by then the engine is warm and smooth. The seatbelt droops over my shoulder, slack across my lap. Brake for the stop sign on the highway. There's a streetlight above it. This is a place. We are in a place now — not pushing a car shape out of the night, but arriving somewhere. Dirty light seeps through the windscreen. The light makes it hard to look out from inside yourself; it makes you see a scene like others do — the Holden nudged against the line, waiting to turn, the girl on the seat with a spray jacket over her pyjamas. I should have brushed my new short hair. I don't want to look unusual, like I'm the story instead of the car. My face is small but there's no one on the seat next to me to compare it to. Check for oncoming traffic. Accelerator, clutch, into second, then smoothly into third. The car picking up speed, the car taking speed from the road, the car stretching out underneath me, stretching like a big cat as it runs the outside lane. All that speed waiting for its opening – the drive shaft powers the axles, the car's ribs accordioned inside its body, hungry for the pedal. Drop your elbows. Drive.

I glance across at the passenger's seat. I imagine I am taking my mother somewhere. I imagine I am driving her away. My mother is not a natural driver. She is separate from the car, adjusting it, nervous at what it might do. Like father man, I can operate all of the car's controls without the words for how it is done travelling across my mind. My skin expands to take in the outer casing of the car. When I tap the dip switch so as not to blind an oncoming vehicle I can feel my eyelids closing around the headlights. I haven't made too many mistakes, although the first time I went night driving in this car, father man's car, I left the handbrake on and drove for nearly an hour with the vehicle in this unhappy condition.

The pointed tip of father man's workshop key brushes

against my thigh as it dangles from the ignition. I don't like to hold or touch a key, or a set of keys, that belongs to another person. I wouldn't ever put a set of keys in my pocket. When I'm turning the ignition on a repair I use a tissue or a rag to hold the key. Females with a perm have their keys in a Glomesh padded purse with gold or silver scales. A boy gives the purse to you. It's what they give you before a ring. I won't ever have the ring. I don't understand why it is twenty-one for getting a card with a key on the front when you get the real key at seventeen. A boy gets the key to his V8; a girl gets the key to her hatchback. If you can make it to seventeen everything opens up then. Once you have the car and the key you don't stay with the family after that.

A corner up ahead. The headlights are painting the road and the bushes on either side. Decelerate. Slow in, a clean change down, the curve of the wheel held to the shape of the road. Trim the line. A good feeling, the matching of machine and corner. If the approach is well handled, somewhere around the clipping point power can be reapplied. The driver must place the car correctly for the turn. The driver must maintain smoothness and stability. Don't stamp the accelerator. Squeeze it open. All that power and movement just there, beneath you.

Check mirrors and road position. Correct use of lanes draws less attention. When the gears are fully played, when the needle hits sixty, that's when I can speak.

'Love is in the air. Love is in the air. Touch me and I will kill you. Love is in the air…' I say to the air above the steering wheel, to the instrument panel with its pretty green glow.

The words bounce against the windscreen and fall to the dash. Cruising now at sixty. A safe speed on this highway at night, with dry conditions, with little traffic. There's enough petrol to go all the way out, and back.

Wednesdays aren't good for school because of softball. I watch my brother get on the bus and then I walk to the tip. I don't take the road. I take the track that's too over-grown for cars in case Darren is out doing firewood. The flies are bad today and the holly banksia is scratchy. The thing about coming across kangaroos in the bush is that they stand up tall with their arms at their sides and their heads very still on their necks like people. They leave it until the last minute to hop away, so there's time for both of you to be scared of the other and to get a good look. The joey breaks first. It's a large joey and all of a sudden it leaps for its mother's pouch. It must be a teenager but it somersaults in, headfirst, so I can see a lot of its tail and its t-square legs and the black underpads of its toes hanging out of the pouch when its mother swivels and bounces off. It's something funny. It's something lovely, really. It's the kind of thing you would like to tell to someone.

The main things at the tip are plastic bags of rotting rubbish and garden hoses and mattresses and broken toys. There are magazines to read. I like most of the smells. When you're in a place that doesn't smell good you can always find somewhere else. Some of the bags of rubbish have secrets inside, but they don't belong to me.

A ponytail isn't a secret. Hair doesn't weigh much and all of its weight is dead. Last night, after everyone had gone to bed, I looked at my ponytail in the kitchen bin. It was splayed over an empty can of corn – damp and sticky. So quickly, it had become rubbish. It took hardly any time at all.

At dinner my mother has her Mills & Boon on the table and there's the television for us. The telephone rings. Father man says not to answer it. My brother washes up; I dry. Then I read a bridal magazine from the tip in my room. I think I'd like to sleep. I try to sleep. There's no firm plan in my mind for sabotage, but after a few hours I climb out of the window and go to the cars. There are always cars to go to. You might just touch them or sit in them, try to sleep a little even, across a bench seat. There's no plan to hurt them, until you do.

It is not a crime if your mouth does it. Soft parts or

hard parts, it's just the same, your two lips making a seal around the hose, your teeth pushing through tired rubber. There are fibres crisscrossed in there, a weak kind of string. The last bit is more grinding than biting. Where it was one firm thing now it hangs doubled, ragged, and you feel sorry about that. Afterwards the oil and the bits of rubber stick to the insides of your cheeks and are foul in your mouth so you need to spit them into the dirt. It's not a crime if your hand does it when your eyes are shut. Blind reaching, blind stroking. Skin on metal. Fingertips tickling bolts, the slackening of the part as its fastenings loosen and then the cool fall of it into the hand. Draped then, quickly, in a rag, or pocketed. The sky will be black after, but a dog won't always be barking. If a dog is barking, even a long way away, you can reach out for each beat so you don't have to listen to the air going in and out of your ribs and the heart over-hot in there too. It's not a crime if your hand does it while you look the other way. You can do it outside. You can do it in the workshop. There are pinholes in the roofing iron for starlight to get through. There are tools with yellow plastic grips that are happy like toys. And you get better at it so your eyes don't even ask to look anymore and your skin isn't nervous. You can use the trowel or a broken piece of star picket to dig a hole and bury the part. Don't bury them too close together – avoid a cluster, give them their own plot. The ground is never too hard for digging. Even with a large part there isn't much excess. The dirt and the stones make room for the part and fit back together again much like before. If you don't look at what you are doing, if you do everything by feel, there are no witnesses. There's the stain on you but that can be cleaned away, and then the only thing that's left is what you felt.

A TRIP

Father man announces a trip. We will sit in the blue Holden. He will drive us in a big arc to a place on the coast on the other side of the country where we can stay in a man's house for free, for three days. Then we will drive home.

Eight days in the car. Three days at the house of father man's friend. Eight days home again.

^

For the trip we each have a plastic shopping bag. Father man says suitcases are useless for the effective packing of a car; too much empty volume. In my plastic shopping bag: four pairs of underpants, four t-shirts, two pairs of shorts, one pair of jeans, a yellow bathing suit I can't wear as it becomes see-through when wet, a purple spray jacket, pyjamas and the *Scientific Publications Holden Workshop Manual*. I don't have a ponytail anymore so I don't need elastics, not since father man cut it off.

^

Preparations for the Holden are extensive. Father man has been put to trouble. I do not, during the time of the preparations, get up at night and go to the cars. I do not pierce a hose or strip the thread of a bolt or loosen any housing or pour beer into the battery. I do not remove a part from the Holden and bury it. I stay in my bed. I read *Seven Little Australians* (the baby is called the General as if he's a horse, the children are stupid but one of them is beautiful) and scratch my mosquito bites.

^

My mother is frightened for her plants. She has made the plants by cutting the tops off potatoes and burying them in dirt. The frilly potato plants hang from the guttering along the edge of the verandah in their baskets of dirt. The night before we go my mother fills plastic drink bottles with water and up-ends them in the dirt in the corner of each basket.

At dawn we troop out of the house with our slept-on

hair, with our plastic bags. An early start. We troop past the mounds of wet soil that has leaked out of the baskets onto the verandah.

'Something to come home to,' father man says.

It's barely light. Headlights will always brighten with engine speed, as long as the alternator voltage is well adjusted.

∧

Father man. My mother. My brother. Myself. Each member of the family has their own window, but you cannot touch the handle. If you wind the window down a gust of air will enter the car and people will object. You cannot object when the other people in the car wind down the window in front of you, or across from you, and you can't object when the driver, who sits in front of you, lights a cigarette and the slipstream from his open window funnels the smoke into your face. Nineteen days ahead.

∧

Food. Petrol. A logbook to record mileage. Road trains. Other cars. Roadkill. My mother's map of Australia is so large she cannot open it when we are moving without obstructing the windscreen.

The car makes the wind and then the windscreen defends us from it.

^

Father man's rules: avoid major roads and highways, don't stop in town, no eating in the vehicle, sound horn repeatedly to push caravaners to the shoulder, don't give way to road trains – hold your speed, hold the road. It doesn't take long before there's nothing to look at. No shops or houses. My mother starts a game of I-spy. My brother chooses f for fart so there's no need to speak. The game is already over.

^

I don't know the name of where we are, but it's time to eat. We sit around the concrete picnic table pecking at a parcel of newspaper. The vinegary chips are best. I let my brother choose then I come in after. Everyone gets their own piece of fish although it's only a fingernail of white under the batter. If you don't eat as fast as they can, or if you can't put hot things straight in your mouth because it will burn, that's tough luck. Father man stands as soon as he's finished and jiggles the car keys. It is annoying for him to be here with us, without his workshop to get away to. My mother wraps up the paper parcel. She wraps it nicely, I think, snug and neat like you might wrap a baby, then she shoos the crows away and pushes the parcel into the rubbish bin.

My brother drinks his lemonade, I drink my Fanta as we walk back to the car. We have driven for a long time but the sky is still full of light. Maybe if we drive fast enough the night will always be ahead of us.

'No glass,' father man says as we open our car doors, so we run back across the gravel to the bin and throw the sweet bottles away.

^

The bush is where we are now. Every Australian road leads into the bush. The stems of plants drill their holes into the soil; the stubble pushes out of the holes on father man's chin. There are holes everywhere shot through with sticks of wheat or needles of hair. What does the sky feel when the wheat stubble rakes against its skin?

^

'Wouldn't you want to drown that?' father man says.

A mother is pushing a large child in a wheelchair along the side of the road. The mother has tied a dishcloth around the child's chin with a ribbon to catch the drool.

What you know about a mother is that she loves you. If you have crutches, or a birth stain on your face, or a melted arm from the kerosene, she'll still love you. A mother doesn't have a choice. Even if you're spastic, if you wet yourself, if you have fits, if you can't shut your mouth and your teeth go yellow, she won't complain or gag or not want to walk with you at the shops.

Father man has slowed down so we can all get a good look at the large child in its wheelchair, but our mother doesn't look. Our mother has her head down; she's searching for something in her red handbag. She's been searching for it all of my life.

^

Follow the white line. Follow the centre line. Out on the highway a dash of white paint marks the edge of each lane. As we come into town there's a dash of white paint and then an orange cat's eye stuck down in between. A dot, then a dash. A dash, then a dot. A dot, then a dash.

^

This town has white concrete wheat silos. You might think they were castles if you didn't know better. A metal ladder is bolted to the outside of the silos for climbing up and jumping off.

^

A black rectangle on top of a faraway yellow hill. Could be a car. Could be a cow.

^

Is the fat lady from next door missing us? Babette will eat the skinks if the fat lady forgets to feed her. The fat lady's sister comes to visit on a Friday – that's the day she's likely to forget. The sister catches the bus. She brings a polystyrene esky on a string. The two women meet on the driveway. They lift their fat legs towards each other and open their fat arms and come together on the gravel. You can see from the side that there is no air between them, that each round part meets its opposite in roundness. They walk back up the driveway together on their high, fat feet. Always the esky swinging from the sister's wrist. What must be kept cool – a dish of jelly, a pair of lamb chops, a part from their girl days that can't be left behind?

∧

Father man needs the municipal toilet. I need it too, but I'm not getting in trouble for holding things up. My mother is asleep. My brother is reading a comic. Father man leaves the keys in the ignition. They stop swaying after a minute or so. I lean forwards, my arm snaking between the seat and the door, and force myself to touch the keys. The door key, the workshop key, three other keys, all hanging with their points towards the floor. A leather cuff hangs too. The edge of it is dark and greasy from where it has swayed backwards and forwards over father man's thigh.

∧

Rain on the windscreen nailing us in. The wiper arm stiff, battering the glass. The dark grey road ahead, above it the dark grey sky with its soft white trim. The road tilts up towards the sky. I wait, breathless, for the bridge, for the giving point where the wheels will leave the road and roll into the sky, but it doesn't come. The road flattens out again; the sky darkens and pulls back. A trick of the dusk.

^

A car is the ideal container for a family. You can be always going to a better place and it keeps everyone stamped down neatly in their seats.

^

Broken brown glass for beer, broken white glass for pop, moss and rocks and ants, flattened bottle tops, prickly bushes with toilet paper streamers, a sports sock, boy shit, dog shit, rabbit pellets, a plastic plate, a pair of green jocks, a vinyl suitcase unzipped – its jaw out of whack – and in among it all, tiny yellow thumb birds, cheeping, apologising to us, at the roadside stop.

^

Sleeping arrangements. Father man and my mother recline their seats using a lever near the floor. They jerk in unison, lurch, settle. My brother stretches out across the back seat. I have the floor. My plastic bag of clothes is soft. I take the clothes out and create two even piles. I use the piles of clothes to raise the floor on both sides of the tunnel created by the transmission hump. Father man has parked us sideways at the roadside stop but the headlights of the cars and trucks on the road still find us. The rear-vision mirror fills with light and then drains away – a long, strong illumination for a road train, a shorter, weaker flash for a car. Why are they going where we have come from? Perhaps I should warn them? Eighteen days ahead.

∧

Packing the right tools for the road requires common sense and forward thinking. Don't take too much or too little. Sandpaper is useful for buffing back the battery terminals, then you can apply some vaseline. Individual parts of bearings must not be renewed separately. If any part of a bearing is faulty, the complete bearing must be replaced.

Father man starts each day by cleaning the grille of the Holden so insects don't get sucked into the engine. He has a brush that he keeps in a plastic bag in the boot. He taps the brush against the tyre rim to clean it afterwards. I think he's happy then. Father man is happiest when he's holding a tool.

The manual in my lap. The road beneath us. A fence rushing past. My brother is asleep with his chin resting on his chest.

There are times when I'm looking at the manual that I can see how everything fits together – the cogs all separate in their airy spaces on the page. All of the parts have the same distance around them. All of the parts are clean. They are made of the same smooth, sheeny substance. A chain is shown dry, without its grease. If the hands are there, the picture is not quite so pure. In *Installing Oil Seal to Crankshaft Flange* the hand spiders over the circular flange, each finger making light contact with its rim. There is some symmetry in how the fingers are arranged, but then there's the stubby thumb, the nail pressed into the bulging flesh below it. A crease of thickened skin heads down to the wrist, a loose web of white skin in the private place between thumb and forefinger. As a covering for the apparatus of the hand, the skin is grimy, irregular. You can see the holes in it, the spaces for things to get in.

In *Exploded View of Front Disc Brake Components*: the piston seal, the piston, the rubber dust seal, the circlip, the shim, the brake pads (there are two; they look like slices of toast), and then, in the same order on the other side, the shim again, the circlip again, the rubber dust seal again, the piston again and finally the piston seal – such a pleasing sandwich of layers and shapes.

There is much to see and learn here, in the manual. It's clear that without brakes, on a hill, a vehicle is a missile — a moving coffin for its driver and anything in its way.

∧

Two cars zoom past in quick succession. The blur of coloured metal, the wind of them bouncing off us, a moan, a pause, another moan.

I wonder if the fat lady could be driven. Imagine an axle put between her teeth. Could she be forced onto the road?

∧

Cars stop in the same places to go to the toilet along the highway. The toilet paper caught on the bushes is yellow from the sun. Men can stop anywhere to piss. Men that wear caps do it on the side of the road. You see them with their shoulders up and their jeans loosened as they hold their dicks. Sometimes they look over their shoulder at you as you drive past. When they are pissing their eyes under their caps are sleepy like a puppy's when its vision is still soft.

Ants enjoy a toilet stop. Here there are black ants with red heads, walking in line, each nest mate carrying its crumb of shit.

∧

There was the time my brother did a big shit in the toilet and he didn't flush, or maybe he did flush but it didn't go away. Father man found it. He said he didn't think it was possible for a child to produce something like that. We were watching *Mash* on television. Men in green pyjamas were doing operations in tents to make us laugh. Our mother was outside with her plants. The back door slammed. We heard father man tell her that her children were animals, that they stank worse than dogs. Our mother came in and stood in front of the television. She was in her weekend clothes, her pink smock top, her blue flares, her Dr Scholl sandals – long slabs of pine belted to her thin feet. I don't know if she had already been to the toilet and flushed, but I knew she shouldn't be talking about the toilet in front of a boy. It was forty degrees. My legs were stuck to the vinyl couch with sweat but I got up and went to the toilet and pushed the button just in case. Dogs don't really stink, but it would have been hard for father man to think quickly of an animal that does.

^

A blue Volvo shimmers, then firms as it overtakes us. In the frozen second before it rushes past, the mouths of its people can be seen moving inside it. A child in the back seat has slid across to the middle where its feet must be banked on the carpeted transmission hump so it can hear the words made in the front and make some of its own.

'The cow is brown,' says their father man from behind the wheel.

'I see a bird,' says the child, its mouth stretched wide like its tonsils are being inspected.

The mother waggles her cap of yellow hair and rubs her legs together. The scritch of her pantyhose leaks out the window and settles on the gravel on the side of the road.

'Soon,' she says, 'we will stop for tea.'

^

A row of foxes tied to a fence, tails up, heads down. A row of shoes tied to a fence by their laces.

^

A long evening on the road. The radio has run out. Father man does not want us to open the doors or windows as we get ready for bed because of mosquitos.

There are no in-between times on the road. We are driving we are sleeping we are eating we are driving we are driving again. Seventeen days ahead.

^

It costs too much money to always eat at a roadhouse. We stop at a small supermarket in the next town so my mother can buy sandwich materials for the picnic basket.

A tiny baby is walking in the supermarket, an Indian baby in a white padded suit with a hood and white knitted shoes that has just learnt to walk. The baby's whole family is in the small supermarket: mother, father, big sister, big brother. They have walked on ahead and are hiding, watching their baby from behind a stack of kitchen towel at the end of the aisle. The baby walks slowly down the middle of the aisle, smaller even than the bottles of drink on the shelf next to it. It doesn't cry or suck its thumb. It looks straight ahead out of its cross brown face. The family laugh softly together and shush each other in case the baby hears as they huddle in their hiding place. The baby's pusher is attached to the hand and the arm of the mother; its wheels run backwards and forwards over the smooth floor of the supermarket. The mother's black hair falls forwards nicely over her face as she is rocked. All of this, while the baby walks its lonely walk.

It could have been stolen, that tiny baby. It could have been crushed and killed. A family will only laugh at cruelty if it knows it is kind.

∧

When you're learning to walk an adult from your family will walk alongside you. The whole of an adult hand is too big for you to hold so the female adult will offer you one part, one finger. You can grip that part with your fat baby's fist to attach your frame to the larger frame of the adult, who knows how to balance, although she will be angry at having to go so slow. All of this will matter later: the fact that you weren't left behind, that you were brought up. In an African tribe twins are considered evil so they put them in pots and leave them in the forest to die. It isn't too deep in the forest where they put the pots of twins so when the other children are out playing and collecting water they can hear the twins crying as they die.

^

The newspaper on the counter at the small supermarket has a picture of a koala that was rescued from a bushfire. Every summer a new koala is rescued from a bush-fire. We'll see photographs of it in the newspapers and on TV for a week or so, until we forget. First the koala will be in a bucket to bathe its singed skin and fur, then sitting in a cage with bandages on its burnt hands. There are blue bandages on its hands if it is male and pink bandages if it is female. The skin of the koala is getting better, its hands are getting better, but it will be dying in its eyes. Only human beings have fancy hands that can grip the hand of another human as they are being brought up. Did it happen so we could link together in a chain with the smallest ones, or did it happen so we could make tools?

In our family father man must look after his hands. The black grease gets into his skin and never gets out but this doesn't matter. It matters when he cuts them. If it's a deep cut he'll get black thread and a sewing needle from the sewing box and stitch it closed himself. It happens at the kitchen table but not while we are eating. Father man's hands put the parts together and take them apart. His hands are where the money comes from.

^

In the car park behind the supermarket father man returns to the wrong car. I see him veer towards another Holden – the same make and model, the same colour blue. I see him insert his key, or try to, in the wrong lock. He hasn't noticed the snapped aerial, the towelling seat cover coming loose in the rear, the balled tissues on the front passenger's floor mat, the copy of *Philately Today* on the dash. I could have called out and saved him.

Forty-one days then, without speech. A flock of birds fall noisily on the bushes that border the car park. A flock of tiny birds trilling to each other. I am walking alongside father man now. I try to motion with my head, to look in the true direction of our car, but father man doesn't see me away from the workshop. Out in the world I am invisible, of less interest than a dog.

I understand father man's confusion. I don't like to

see the Holden in a car park. I don't like to see it shoulder to shoulder with another make of car, its tyres potted inside the painted lines. I don't like large car parks where there are too many cars, rows and rows and rows of cars – it is sad to see them docile, waiting for a family to remember them, to return and fit themselves inside.

When a car is born it has all the promise of movement – a spin of the wheel and the tyres will dance it in any direction. It is only when it is taken home that a car understands it is sentenced to life on the road.

∧

Yesterday, on average, if I counted to ten there would be a house or a gate, or a letterbox. Today I have counted to 817 with no sign of human life.

The road ahead is not for my eyes to open onto. From the rear seat the front screen is obstructed like at the movies, where the back of the heads of tall people block out the horse's legs if it's John Wayne, or the deep sea if it's *Jaws*. My eyes are for the side. Sitting behind father man I can look down all the driveways we could turn into. A set of gates, a cattle grate beneath them, a white drum for mail, sometimes a sign if the place is a stud and there is something to tell about the sheep and the cows.

Some of the big farms – they might be called stations – have paddock cars left near the front gate for children to drive up to the house and down to the road for school. When there is a whole family of children the biggest one does the driving. The biggest brother or sister could kill the smaller brothers and sisters by driving into a tree or a dam, but they don't, and they don't wait until the smaller children have gotten out of the car so they can drive away somewhere. They could do that; it wouldn't be hard. But they don't.

^

Father man is driving with his right arm out of the window. His left arm steers. All morning now we've tracked the river. How friendly to keep time with this happy road of water flowing by our side.

^

My mother's eye drops have leaked in her handbag and *Chateau in the Palms* is wet through. While we are stopped at the roadside stop my mother puts the book on the roof of the Holden to dry. Every time a car zooms past the pages flicker in the wind as if the speeding vehicle is reading the book very, very fast. My mother is lucky; she has good timing, because we're not far down the highway when it starts to rain.

^

I remember playing in the storm drain with my brother after a week of rain. We started by running up the road and throwing sticks and leaves into the water and chasing them down until they became snagged. I think the game was to see whose sticks went furthest. A few times when my brother's stick was slower or became snagged he switched to following my stick. I clapped for him when his stick – the stick that had been mine – went over the imaginary finishing line. When cars came and we had to get off the road my brother waited to see which side of the road I would go to and then he went to the other side.

For the next game we dragged boulders into the drain and diverted the water across the road. In the deepest part of the drain above our dam the water was a clean, cold muscle, but after the water had coursed around the boulders that we had rocked out of the soil, and through the dirt that clung to them, it was weak and brown. The weak brown water spilled across the road in a puddle.

All that day I copied what my brother did. Not exactly – I watched what he did and then calculated what was a half of it. If he chose a big boulder and started rocking it to loosen it from the soil I found a boulder half its size. Once my brother's boulder was free he kicked it so it rolled down into the drain, running away just before the splash. My boulders weren't heavy enough to roll on their own; they lacked weight and impetus. I had to squat down beside them and pat them along. Our hands were coated with mud, and our jeans too, around the knees and higher up where we had wiped ourselves.

'It's like the trenches,' I said to my brother.

He nodded but then he turned away. It wasn't right of me to try and hook him like that. I had forgotten myself – I had become too excited and I wished I could take it back.

We climbed the orange trees at the front of the block and watched the brown puddle leak over the road. We didn't say so, but we thought the water would make the next car that drove along skid and crash. My brother ate five of the miniature oranges. Runt fruit, we called them. I ate two. Then we sat, full of sweet juice, listening for the sound of a car approaching – maybe even a bus.

I don't know why I remember this. I don't know if I'll always remember it. Perhaps, later on, I won't need to remember it anymore and something else will be there instead.

ᴧ

At Caiguna father man stops for petrol and cigarettes. A Ford stands cooling at the bowser opposite. It can't have come far on these roads, its bright work still shining. Father man goes in to pay and emerges with a fresh pack of cigarettes. He checks that our eyes are seeing him, then he pretends to reach for the doorhandle of the Ford as if he has mistaken one car for another.

'Just ragging,' his mouth says.

Is this play? Should we have smiled? He opens the correct door, the door to the blue Holden. He settles himself in the seat, lights his cigarette and speaks at the back seat.

'Ah, there's Stupid, and there's Stupider,' he says.

Children are only half a person so it's right that we must share the word.

^

The manual on my lap. My brother asleep with his mouth open and his fringe puffing out in front every time he breathes.

My man's hands are in thirteen of the twenty-seven photographs in the workshop manual for the Holden, but never in an exploded view. An exploded view is to show the spaces between the parts and how they fit together. My man's hands model the parts in situ – show how they are to be manipulated. My man's hands are pale and clean. They point, touch, grasp, turn, hold. They show scale and direction. Here is the diaphragm; here is the valve, the economy jet… My man's hands suggest, by the tension or softness of his flesh, the force required for the task.

81

They demonstrate to every man who reads the manual that the procedures for installation, for dismantling, for tensioning, for alignment are all achievable with a little patience and, of course, with his own pair of hands.

It is good to stare at the place in the photograph where the flesh of the fingers meets the part. This way the part loses its edge. The softness of the hand un-engineers the part. My man wears no ring on any of his fingers. My man's hands are not old, but they are not the hands of a boy. My man's hands don't force a part to separate from another – they coax. It is the hand that corrupts, not the part.

In the manual each cog is separated on the page. Here is the hand fingering the accelerator pump. The pieces of the pump float on the papered air. The numbers, the instructions, the photographs are in front and behind the hands and the parts. The hands have no body – no arms or legs, no thigh in overalls to rest slackly against. The parts have no chassis, no cabin dragging its stuttery shadow down the road. The parts are designed to come together. A flange, a rim – flat metal against flat metal – a valve, a spindle, a pin, a bolt, the housing and the housed. In the manual everything is straight. Everything is clean. A pure view.

Tap, tap, tap. The week after father man arrived he tapped the timber handle of his hammer against my head. 'Like to like,' he said. 'Wood meets wood.'

In *Removing Circlip from Lower Ball Joint* my man holds a pair of pliers like he is gripping the wings of a bird. The pliers stab the circlip with their beak. A few black hairs at the wrist of my man's hands. I can see his palm, the pillow of flesh beneath his thumb. I can see his fingernails, neat and shiny like postage stamps.

In the night my man's hands will graze my cheeks, will reach behind my head, will grasp my neck, the hairs at the nape of my neck, and tug, not sharply so it will rip, but enough to wake the skin underneath the hair. My man will do it the way that I do it to myself, but it will not be my weak girl's hands – it will be his grown man's hands. The hands he has given to me in the manual.

^

The road is chalked here. A section of it is scribbled with measurements and arrows – instructions for a road crew to come back later for repairs.

I like it on the cop shows when they draw a line on the pavement around a dead body in chalk. Most people in America get shot. You don't see the body. You see the white chalk on the black pavement. The fat lady next door says it's a good day when you wake up in the morning and there's no chalk line drawn around you. I know what she means. I watch the cop shows too. The chalk line is a stencil for a body without its flesh, without its parts. It wouldn't work in the outback. If you were shot or stabbed in the outback there is no hard pavement, there's just the dirty paddocks full of stubble and animal shit. There's no firm surface to press against.

A girl that is young has just the one edge, just the one long outside line between herself and the world. When she starts to wear a bra and the breasts and the black hair must be hidden, the life of parts begins. Skirts and dresses are a factor of it. You can't draw a chalk line around a body when it's wearing a skirt. Some of the lines won't be true. It is always possible to draw a line around a man. There's the edge of him; there's him on one side of the chalk, the world on the other, but not for a woman, or a girl like me.

^

Father man has the road in his hands and the Holden that adheres to it and the stream of air it pushes against, and us strapped inside. He passes us from palm to palm between two socks, because, after being parked in the sun, the steering wheel is as hot as an oven tray.

Mother says, 'don't park here, find some shade,' but there isn't any shade close to the shop. When mother has the wheel she parks head-on to a tree with the bonnet pushed right against it like the car is a horse hitched outside a bank. Our rear end jutting out onto the road.

We get out of the car and file down the road to the shop for a pie with sauce and an orange juice. Then we file back up again. Road trains pass us and spit gravel against our legs. Nobody wants the pulp that sinks to the bottom of the orange juice. It is a relief to get back into the car.

^

Dusk. A different type of cicadas here, or it could be frogs. Father man has a last piss on the bushes at the roadside stop. He locks the car doors. I can see my brother's elbow working away above me. He is picking the tops off his pimples. The road sounds get quieter through the night. Sixteen days ahead.

^

There's always a fly trapped inside, hitting itself against the glass. Its buzzing gets louder as we drive. You can squash the fly with your hand or you can wind the window down a fraction and shoo it towards the gap. If it has been in the car for long enough perhaps it will be released to a new fly-country with a different fly-language? Maybe it will be happy there, but more likely it will be killed.

At home I like to make sure that I'm not on the verandah much, but it was good to watch the skinks eat the flies, their tongues snapping out blind and sticky. It wasn't hard to collect a handful of flies from the windowsills, the black tangle of them – eyelash legs, church-window wings. Sometimes a fly was on its back, but mainly they were tilted over. So light, a fly, a whole life too light to register in my hand. What I didn't know was that my mother had been spraying with the extra-strength Mortein. I fed the Mortein flies to the skink family for lunch for a week before a little poison became a lot, became too much. All the skinks died except for the big one. Maybe it was the father? It knew my smell or shadow and came out from under its rock ready to feed. I didn't have any flies. I picked it up by the tail, the way you shouldn't. It was sleek and plump. Its ear slit glared open like the eye of a needle. It didn't cry out but there was blood on my hand when I flicked its tail away.

I remember this because earlier that day I had been cleaning the parts in kerosene under the trees. I was putting the clean parts back on the bench in the workshop when father man called out to me from the pit. Father man was in the pit underneath the Holden. I had crept past on my way to the bench, but he must have seen my ankles.

He told me to bring a spanner down the ladder into the pit. Then he told me to go up again and bring a rag.

^

Between Eucla and Yalata the blue Volvo comes past again. The mother is in the back now with her yellow hair squashed against the door strut. The small one is in the front but its mouth is closed. The father man is driving under a hat. He's had enough. Their three mouths are closed, just like ours.

∧

Further on there's a man with a broken-down motorbike on the side of the road. The dirt is red here and the motor-cyclist's white t-shirt is pink from where he's been lying in the dirt. He's given up trying to fix the motorbike. He's sitting on his leather jacket with his black helmet between his legs and his thumb pointed out at us as we drive past. There are a few tools scattered in the dirt around the back wheel of the motorbike that he hasn't bothered to pack away. When it is clear that we are not going to stop he flips his hand over and sticks his middle finger up angrily.

You can have a motorbike or you can have a family. You can't have both. The thing you need to do about the motorbike man stuck on the side of the road is to never think about him and his broken-down motorbike again.

∧

I brought an old golf trolley home from the tip once and gave it to my brother. Things with wheels are prized at the tip. A father will take the wheels from an old pram and build a go-kart for his boy. He'll tell the boy to be careful and take a photograph as the boy rides the go-kart in front of the house. The mother might come out too and watch for a bit in her apron, or call them in for tea. Who knows what they eat, but they drink white milk out of tall glasses.

My brother dragged the rusty golf trolley to the top of Struttle Road hill and strapped himself to it. He wove the vinyl strap that's meant to go around the bag of clubs through the belt loops of his Lee jeans. My brother was the cab and the chassis of his golf trolley car, but the weight of him was not enough to fasten the wheels to the road.

The snapped bone inside my brother's leg was hidden by the flesh around it. What to do first – unthread him from the broken trolley or wipe his wet cheeks with my sleeve?

When the cast came off my brother's leg all the muscles had gone. His leg was wasted and unreliable. An unused machine becomes brittle and is subject to rust, but its parts never waste.

Thinking about my brother's wasted leg made me worried for my face. Could not speaking make my face sink like with old people who have lost their teeth? I began some exercises in front of the mirror, whispering a song – either a nursery rhyme or Kate Bush. Then I expressed surprise and pretended to greet someone fondly, my lips puckered for a kiss. Lastly, I thought of something good that a smile could feed on. When the smile didn't come I lifted my lips and bared my teeth instead. It's what dogs do in warning. It's a simple way of saying: *I'm dangerous, don't come near.*

^

A road sign tells us a bridge is up ahead so we'll pay attention, so we don't get surprised. You could live under a bridge. Under a bridge could be a sort of house. If it was a wide bridge you'd sleep right under the middle so the rain didn't get in at the sides. There aren't any cupboards but you could take bricks out of the pillars and store things behind them. Then you could go off in the daytime and you and your things would always be safe.

^

The inside of a burnt tree could be a house, except it is full of charcoal. A shed is the best house, or a mechanic's work-shop or an outside laundry. It makes sense to sleep in the pit in the workshop and climb up and down the ladder to your bed. If you had a cat or a dog you'd have to lift them up or down, or maybe, with time and practice, they could learn the ladder. My brother put me in the fridge once. It's not that I was especially small. It was a big fridge and I got in the salad crisper at the bottom and scraps of lettuce that were wet and see-through stuck to my legs.

^

My mother is reading *The Silken Trap*. When it is finished she wraps it in a plastic bag and puts it in the boot of the Holden. Then she is reading *With This Ring*.

When you see a knife-beaked bird, like a kooka-burra, think of it inside an egg. It will sweeten you to imagine the bird as a chick, cramped and scruffy-feathered in its tight white egg. When you see a man, think of a baby in its snug blue blanket. When you see a snake, think of a pink worm in wet soil.

^

The gravy is hot so I'm not fast enough to eat my pie. It doesn't take long before it's too long off the road. Nobody waits for a girl. If you don't do something fast enough you have to run or you have to pretend you have done the thing so you don't hold everyone up.

^

Here's a town. The local football ground has red dirt instead of grass. Two tall white goalposts in the middle, a shorter one on either side. The Australian family. It must be training because a clump of men chase a ball, but nobody is wearing a uniform. The ball flies up in the air and a black man climbs on the back of a white man like a lizard up a tree. It's to take a mark, so nobody minds.

∧

The roadside stop isn't in the right place tonight so we park on the hard shoulder and get ready to sleep. Father man locks the car doors. My mother pushes her bra straps off her shoulders. She puts a cardigan over her face and says goodnight. Father man has a last cigarette. I can hear the dry skin of his lips sticking and unsticking to the damp white paper.

I might have too much spit for kissing. What's better for kissing – a dry tongue or a wet tongue? When I was small and I had a cold my brother said his spit was medicine. I opened my mouth and he spat a warm ball of it into me. I can't remember if it worked.

I don't know how to shut myself off in the car tonight. I'd like to go for a walk on the road. I'd like a torch to read the manual. I shut my eyes and make the pages come up behind them. If I concentrate hard I can read it in my mind.

Modelling the parts has tuned my man's hands to weight and tension. He can feel how the fabric of my jeans tightens where my thighs are fullest. There are empty belt loops for him to finger. There's the ridge that marks the elastic of my underpants where it grips the top of each leg. *Undoing Waist Stud* has several stages. It starts with grasping and squeezing – the thumb against the pubic bone, the fingers between the legs, the unzipping of the zip. Before the waist stud is undone the fingers trace the edge of the waistband, opening up a space between the fabric and the skin. The undoing of the stud is quick, simply done. My man's hands have good weight and warmth; they cause no upset to my skin. I don't know if other females have a trail of fine hairs down their belly, or such a brushy thickness of it between their legs. Because of this what happens next happens through the cotton of my underpants, although the hair is always snaking out and the fabric can easily be pushed aside. With his thumbs, with the very tips of his fingers, my man's hands separate the folds to stroke the collar of the hooded pin at the centre join of me. Then he pumps its tip. In an engine this mechanism is a primer, a way of establishing a necessary flow.

I turn over and rearrange my t-shirt-pushed-inside-my-yellow-bathing-suit pillow. Fifteen days ahead.

^

One sheep in a paddock of dull grey sheep has its head in a hollowed-out tree stump. Is it a smart sheep, or a dumb sheep?

^

I have a big appetite for toast but there's only one piece in the paper envelope. The girl doing till in the roadhouse has gold chains in her ears. Chain links fold back on themselves under force. How did the girl push the thin chains through the flesh of her earlobe? A safety pin, a compass, a needle? She mustn't feel the gritty bit of chain dragging at the inside meat of her ear anymore, but she must have felt it the first time. Each road train trailer has safety chains to connect it to the trailer in front. It's only in case the coupling fails. Sometimes, when a trailer has been unhitched, you'll see the chains resting slackly on the ground. Each fat link looks like a piece of dog shit – part of a chain of shit that's been laid down as the dog got bored and walked away while the shit kept coming.

∧

The road is just the road now. There are no historic monuments or animal sanctuaries or adventure parks. There is no minigolf, no viewing platforms or waterfalls. When there are, you never stop at them. There is the name of the town you left and the name of the town you will arrive at. You might as well be driving across the face of a map.

∧

Sad trees along the roadside dripping wet. The rain chips, pins, wobbles, breaks and smatters across the windscreen. Again. Again. Again. Only the broken rain hits the passenger's window, then it drips away for the road and grass to have. A clump of brown sheep, tired, despised. The railway line beside the road pulls us towards it and then away. The rusty tracks, always twinned, always high and proud of the grey stone bed beneath them. What a fine road they make to scrape along.

^

A road sign shows a mother duck looking back over her shoulder at a line of ducklings as she crosses the road. You never actually see that and nobody would stop if they did.

^

Father man is in charge of the five primary controls – the throttle, the footbrake, the handbrake, the gear lever, the steering wheel – and the nine secondary controls – the choke, the ignition, the starter, the indicators, the lights, the dip switch, the horn, the windscreen wiper and windscreen washer. He has two hands and two feet to operate fourteen controls. No large forces are needed. Most of the action is in the head. Father man assesses the road, the environment, the conditions and the car, making constant, minute adjustments. He knows how to keep the car away from other cars on the safe side of the road. He knows how to manoeuvre through small spaces and park without incident. From this it can be seen that he has the best interests of the family at heart.

When father man gets behind the wheel the car becomes included in his body, so that the outer edge of the car becomes his outer edge, even with us inside.

∧

A sign with the South Australian road toll on it. They updated it every year from 1970 to 1975. I doubt it means there haven't been any deaths since 1975. It's a small sign with an advertisement for Wing Chin Chinese restaurant in the corner. I think they just ran out of room.

∧

The manual again. In *Checking Oil Pump Impeller Radial Clearance*, the oil pump is high in the picture. It is almost life-sized. The hand grasps the pump in a relaxed grip. The fingers are curled, almost touching, resting expectantly next to each other. There is a black line between each finger. Just near the knuckle joint, in the split between the first and second finger, the flesh bulges a little, like a stomach, or a cheek. The knuckle skin is smooth and glassy like nipple skin, but I've only ever touched my own. What you are looking for when you insert the feeler gauge is a free fit with minimum clearance. The spindle must be flush with the propeller at all times.

∧

My mother is cleaning her teeth at the handbasin in the petrol station toilet. We know we are in the ladies because there's a smiling Spanish dancing girl on the door. The sun has gone down even further when we come out. Just a few hours of driving in the dark, then I will be on the floor of the car again. My brother falls asleep first, then my mother, then father man. The car smells of bananas but there's enough air down here to get a girl through the night.

^

There is a place for a girl, but it is not in a room, is not in a house, is not in a bed, is not in a garden, it is not in water, it is not in sunlight or under the branches of trees. The place for a girl is in a car. The girl in the car is on a road. The surface of the road is glittering. Nobody, not even the girl, knows if the car is travelling through the speckled stars of the black sky or across the chipped stones of the black road.

My brother burps. An owl hoots from a roadside tree. Fourteen days ahead.

^

Scaly-footed young magpies own the Rotary park and picnic stop. They show us their beaks and make their demands.

^

Here's a road train, an eleven-wheeler. It says *long vehicle* on the mudguards. The road train is in front of us. It kinks its hips around the bend, the skirt of its trailer following on behind.

^

When we leave the car to eat or piss or to stretch our legs we are drawn straight back to it. At the roadside stop we fan out from our car but we always keep it in sight. You never approach the empty waiting car of another. You never touch the empty waiting car of another, even though the car itself can't feel. Doors opening. Doors closing. Everyone has their corner. Our legs must be starting to wither, but why walk when you can drive?

^

You can tell from behind, from the way that they drive, when a driver is wearing a hat inside the car. They are never a good driver. Wearing a hat inside the car means they do not understand the meaning of the car. It's usually someone on their own. A family in the same car shares the shelter of the roof. The car becomes the family hat.

^

My mother asks me if I am having some trouble talking. She asks me if I have a sore throat.

^

I miss the night driving. I miss pushing a car through the dark with my foot on the petrol, my hands on the wheel. I might cry today. I don't know why, but I have to be careful so the tears don't get out. I should be happy. Here I am, a girl on the road with her family. A girl on the road who is safe.

∧

It must be the afternoon because here are some children coming home from school. They are waiting to cross the highway opposite the petrol station. The girls hold their schoolbags in front of them so the wind from the road doesn't blow up their checked dresses. There's an automotive repair workshop next to the petrol station. A mechanic sits drinking a can of Coke on a kerosene drum underneath the rolled-up roller door. Father man is cleaning our windows with the window-cleaning stick. For a second my view of the mechanic is sudsy, and then it is clear. The mechanic must have been a schoolchild once. Now he sits sucking on his can and you can see straight up the leg of his shorts where there are two eggs squashed in a red bag and the white stalk of his dick.

A tool is an expression of its user. It looks raw, what the mechanic has between his legs. Like it has only just been born. An afterbirth, or an afterthought.

The schoolchildren go into the petrol station. I think they'll buy Cheezels and then they'll go home.

∧

When we pull back out onto the road it's still the wheat belt so I close my eyes and think about Sharon's tyre boy. I imagine that he's mine. I imagine that I meet him at lunchtime. We cross the highway. I have a fifty-cent coin in the hip pocket of my jeans; I buy the boy a pie. The boy peels back the plastic top of the sauce with his black fingers. When he bites into the pie, mince drips out and he swoops down on it and gulps at the hot meat. A smear of it is on his face now. I want to wipe it away like a mother does, but you have to be wary of that. It's best that they don't ever think you are the boss of them. The brown meat on the boy's face is drying to a dark crust. I don't know what we might do next so I imagine it is evening. We've driven past so many motels now, but I've never been inside one.

Here we are then, just as the night turns grey. I decide to give the tyre boy a ute because he only has a bicycle. I give the boy a white HR ute with three on the tree. When the boy changes gear he does something funny with his elbow – like a cat boxing with its paw. I'm sitting next to the boy on the bench seat with my elbow out the window. My arm is brown, the brown you can only get from going to the beach. The boy drives onto the concrete apron in front of the Best Western motel with hair dryers and colour television and a hatch next to the door for breakfast to be slid through. Six steps between the ute and the room, the engine of the mini fridge taking over with a hum, hum, hum, now that the ute is resting quietly outside. There's a double bed with a bedspread in seatcover chenille. There are glove boxes on both sides of the bed and twin hinged silver ashtrays that flip out to crush your smokes into. There's a mirror with headlights on each side of the bedhead to see by. The television is on a wheeled tray in front of us. The boy presses the ignition on the wooden dash and selects the channel. With television we don't have to go through all the dead places to get somewhere. The picture on the television screen assembles and we are behind the wheel in San Francisco looking out at tall wooden houses crowded together on a steep hill, the water of the bay ahead, a glimpse of the shouldered bridge, the pale, patched road falling away in front of us. The tyres screech as the car hurtles across an intersection, is airborne for a second, then slams back down against the road. It can't be good for the suspension. Our car chases the car ahead in the way dogs chase cats. It's only for entertainment – everyone knows they will never catch each other.

The boy lies next to me on the double bed. He's making revving noises behind his teeth.

'I'll take you for a spin,' the boy says and he rolls over and pops the press-studs on my denim shirt.

I need some time here to imagine more stuff that he might do to me, so I take the roof off the Best Western motel. When you look down from above there is a line of bedroom boxes side by side for couples and a line of car parks for cars to rest from the road. You can be safe from the lounge room and the kitchen when you are on the road – there's no need for rooms to be a family in.

Here's a crane-view of a boy and a girl on the bed in every room, just like me and the boy from the automotive, except that this me I'm looking down on has brown skin all over and long yellow hair and good jeans that aren't handed down from my brother.

Back in the motel room now. I'm lying down on the bed and the door is open – there's just the flyscreen between us and the white ute. If I turn my head on the pillow I can see past the boy's shoulder and out the door. The ute is beautiful through the hazy veil of the flyscreen. In a motel you can be gone first thing in the morning; you can be gone as soon as you put the key in the ignition and turn it home.

∧

A pink nightdress of dirt gets up off the flat and swirls towards us – up down, up down, and then it peters out.

You might think a family in a car would see the same things, but that's only if they look through the same window. Four people, four individual winding panes of glass, and the family screen in front. Nobody mentions the pink wind but I know I'm not the only one that saw.

^

Paddocks and paddocks of broccoli trees with black bark. They are native trees – they don't make fruit and nobody planted them. They grew up injured all together.

^

The road is always in me now. We are always going past the same dreary scenes. In westerns they ride in front of the same cardboard rocks glued to the same painted canyon. A cowboy horse can become an Indian horse just with a change of saddle blanket, although sometimes they scruff up the mane.

^

We had a different television set in the time before. I remember my brother walking up to the screen to pat a dog with a long snout. There is an adult-sized face reflected in the screen as my brother holds out his hand towards the dog. I was still a baby then. Was my mother in the room? Perhaps it was someone else?

∧

My mother is opening and closing her red handbag. She unzips her purse and counts her loose change. She likes to pay for things in coins rather than notes if she can. My mother looks over at my brother and me in the back seat and starts to sing. She sings, 'row, row, row your boat...' Father man lights a cigarette. Life is but a dream...

∧

Coming into a town. A greyhound track next to a wrecking yard. All quiet. Not a dog or a person in sight. The track where the dogs race is edged in bent sheets of corrugated iron. I think it happens at night. There are big floodlights hanging overhead and an advertisement for beer and charcoal chicken near the entrance. *Enjoy Your Night at the Dishlickers*, it says and there's a picture of a happy greyhound with a long pink tongue cheekily licking its chops.

I often see the man who lives two streets from us on Bonnington Road walk his greyhounds in the mornings. Five dogs trot beside him, lean against his legs, lift their caged snouts into the air of the day. The man walks them on the gravel path. Darren tells father man that when the greyhounds don't win at their races, when the man from Bonnington Road doesn't want them anymore, he has a hammer in his shed to kill them with.

My first choice is the lilac, next the fawn with the

drooping ear tips, then the brindles. The black is last. One morning I saw the black dog quiver when the dog man ashed his cigarette over its back. I saw the black dog's skin shrink and pull tight, then prickle and bead up along the knuckles of its spine.

The dog man's hands cannot end the dogs. His hammer can. Perhaps it is a clean feeling to break a skull and feel the glue behind it? The flies are always quieter after you've done the thing you had to do.

I went in on a moonless night from the back, across the creek, through the bush, to avoid the gravelled driveway and the windows of the house. The dog man's house is brick with a belt of hedge around it. The dog shed is at the rear. A chicken wire fence bulging between stakes, a bolt on the shed door to be coaxed from its keep. Streetlight beamed through the holes in the tin roof, silvering the cages of the sleeping dogs. Fear that the dogs would wake and bark. It was a comfort to hold the torch. When there's a stick-up on *Hogan's Heroes* and the German soldier drops his gun, the television lingers on the hand so you can see the sadness in the fingers as the gun drops and falls away. That was how my hand felt about the torch. I put the torch down on the bench, next to the hammer. The lilac dog stood up then and tottered to the corner of its pen to squat but nothing came. It yawned and circled then lowered itself back down to sleep. The two brindle dogs were penned together, were asleep on their sacks together, so it wasn't possible to see where each of them began and ended.

The dog man had wiped the hammer's crime from its face. The silver disc was spotless. It could have been a stud or a button, a token in a board game, a wristwatch whose hands had fallen free. The blood was on the rag. When the rag dried it had lost its softness, but that's where the blood had ended up, that's where it had to stay.

The rag remembered it was cloth, remembered how to rip. No dog woke. There were enough strips of rag to wrap the hammer three times. The dog man's hammer came out looking like a baby. He'd find it in the morning. There it would be, on the bench, ready for its cradling.

^

I miss the smell of my bed. I miss the sound of father man's beer fridge clearing its throat on the back verandah. Do I miss the sabotage? Do I miss getting up in the night, putting my hands in an engine, deciding which part to take or hurt?

^

A flat tyre. Father man has to unload the contents of the boot to reach the spare and the wheel brace and the jack. He's angry about all the useless shit we have brought with us. He's angry about having to move the plastic bags. My mother lifts the picnic basket up off the dirt and holds it against her hip as if it's precious, as if she's worried it might get left behind. My brother holds his ball. A few cars pass us on the road. The people in the cars are looking at us, my mother with her headscarf, with her round knees and pink shorts, my brother bouncing his ball in the dirt.

The correct wheel rotation to prolong the life of the tyres starts with the spare in the boot. Move the spare to back left. Drive. Move spare to front left. Drive. Move spare across to front right – this is a big move as the tyre is now on the other side of the car. Drive. Move spare to back right, then return spare to boot. When the spare is in the boot it is flat like a lozenge. It has done what it was meant to do. It is all sealed away. It can rest now.

Father man concentrates on the task at hand, but the fury in his back and arms and shoulders signals to any helpful passing car that it's better not to stop.

My mother asks everyone what their favourite meal is. Only my brother answers: fish fingers, orange jelly and ice cream.

∧

What if you were to choose a tool to love? Not a different one every day or every week, but the same tool for your whole life? Father man would be a hammer. My mother would be a rag. I would be a knife. The knife handle, the knife blade, the knife tip is nothing without a hand to hold it. A knife is deaf, of course – it is all tongue but no talk. It is momentum, forward motion; a knife has no brake, it is treachery and misery. A knife is the most sordid of tools. Cut and run, slash and spill. My brother would be string.

∧

Last month my brother said his tooth hurt. We were watching television together. He is frightened of the dentist and I knew that he had cried. He opened his mouth and I saw his tonsils – two red bells hanging down. He said he'd give me fifty cents to pull the tooth out with the doorknob and a length of cotton. He showed me the coin. It had the same tissue lint on it as in our mother's purse. My brother sat on his bed. He couldn't open his mouth very wide. Strings of white saliva stretched between his jaws. The first time I tensioned the cotton with the door closed, so it wasn't taut enough to pull. The cotton was green when it should have been white. The second time, I opened the door, wrapped the thread tight around the handle, and then, without warning, kicked the door shut. The difference between a grown-up and a child is knowing when the blood will come. An adult would have tied a bib around the boy's neck, or made him put on old clothes. When it comes mixed with warm saliva, blood is a bubbly, hopeful pink.

That same night, while I listened to my brother snivelling through the wall, a truck ditched into the arrester bed. We didn't hear it happen. I don't know what sort of noise it made, or if the sound would have been loud enough to carry up the hill to the house. The ditching was reported on the news. A wet road. An empty road train returning from the eastern states lost its brakes on the descent. It was picking up speed – a missile waiting to slam its hardness into an oncoming car, or a highway-side cottage, or a lady with a pramload of babies, or a man out walking a sweet old dog – but the experienced truck driver took the centre of the road and steered and coaxed the runaway wheels around each curve and bend, waiting for the arrester bed he knew was up ahead. It was a good-news story. The next day there was footage of a crane mounted on the back of another truck pulling the road train out of the gravel, and the gravel dripping out of the engine and the cabin like orange hail. There was footage of the sign: *Truck Arrester Bed Ahead*. The reporter said the truck driver didn't even have time to wind up the window. The driver wasn't shown. Perhaps he was in hospital? Perhaps the gravel flooded the cab and pushed all around him and into his ears and his nostrils and the sockets of his eyes? I would like to know from him how the rush of the descent felt – did the heavy cab and engine drag the trailers hitched behind, or did the trailers bunch up and push the cabin on?

^

A dead magpie on the road salutes me with its wing, an armpit of blood and broken feathers. Sometimes, when it's fresh, the magpie family will be gathered in the other lane, paying their last attendance.

^

I don't know where the birds go at night. Are they safe in the dark? Father man locks the doors. I watch the first star of the night out of the window for a long time. Eventually the world turns and the star is gone. I haven't cleaned my teeth. For some reason I lied about that, not that there's ever been kissing. Thirteen days ahead.

^

I dream of a car that flies. The sky car hovers free of the road. All of its parts are flying in unison. There are no highways up here; the sky car pierces a cloud. The cloud's stuffing explodes into the atmosphere. Infinite speed is possible. My sky car has television and a hair dryer and a biscuit tin. There is a first-aid kit mounted on the door strut next to the seatbelt but when you open it, it makes milkshakes. There is no need to sit and watch the road.

I don't know where the power comes from. There is no petrol tank – perhaps the power comes from me?

^

In this town pink and grey galahs peck at the watered grass around the municipal pool and squat old ladies in white bowls dresses walk up the street together. There's a pub and a cafe and a bank and a Chinese restaurant with a red and gold sign. Some of the bowls ladies have blue hair, some have lilac hair, but most have white hair. It must be nice to stand on the green carpet grass but I wouldn't want to wear the pantyhose or put my hands around the cold black ball. Some of these ladies might be sisters. Even when they are old, sisters can be next to each other. It doesn't seem like a sad life.

^

There are times that we have to stop so my brother can play with his ball. Except the further in we get the less he wants to play with it. On the other side of Hay my brother kicks his ball over a fence and into a paddock. We drive away and leave it there.

^

Just the road and the car slowing down even though there isn't a corner or an intersection ahead. We have driven through the screen of the day into the place that a crash has made. Why here? The road is straight, no hazards, but there's a bridge nearby – perhaps it is implicated?

Mother says, 'don't look.' She says, 'look away,' but father man slows so we are crawling, ambling past, and what to do but feast on it? We never see inside the body; we never see the foundations from which we are made. But here is a red car that has torn into a green car. They are resting now, but all around them is the force of the tear. The red car is puckered through its middle, seats slumped forwards, the steering wheel jutting rudely on its black stem. The road displays its takings: an ashtray shaken free, still rocking on its hinges, a yellow plastic bag, a red biro, strips of black vinyl, sunglasses, a rubber floor mat, some wrapping paper, tissues, an empty packet of Twisties, a can of ginger beer, unidentifiable small pieces of plastic that might be part of the same item.

The car's body is misshapen, hard to look at, but the broken glass on the road glitters and entertains. Why are some colours more violent than others? The fleck, the shatter, the spray of jagged glass. Then back to the red car again, its gills, guts, tendons, the tufts of cushion fat ripped free. Petrol dripping from the red car's flanks, petrol gleaming in wavy pinks and greens, slipping across the road. Moving past it now, a stretch of empty road, a little glass underneath our tyres sounding like biscuits being crumbled, several onlookers standing, onlooking, then we are approaching the green car, which is tilted, playfully, on its roof. The glass cabin of the green car is intact against the road like a multi-sided aquarium. All of this is aftermath. There's no hint of where the cars were — in which direction they were travelling. Was the first touch the only impact? Did they skid together and then apart? Did they travel the road in chaos together, torn panel to torn panel? The green car has a list of pleated wounds cut into its bonnet. Does the road cut, at speed?

My mother moans at the back of her throat because the door of the green car is hanging loose from its shoulder, and the inner side of it, across the window and down to where the handle of the window winder is, is sprayed with smeary orange blood. Because the door of the car is upside down the blood seems to be dripping upwards, as if it is seeking release in the sky. How stupid for the wheels to be free from the road. Four small black circles, like licorice allsorts, decorating the air.

I forgot to say about the people. A grey blanket covers a body on the hard shoulder. It would have been nicer to move it off the road. A woman with messy hair and her head in her hands sits in the front seat of a van that has stopped. It isn't her van because she sits as if she's on a seat in someone's kitchen, or at a barbecue, not in a vehicle. I think I see blood, in between where her hands are caged to her head, but it could be lipstick. There's movement in the deep ditch along the far side of the road, behind the red car. I can see the tops of two heads: a bald head, a sandy-haired head. The faces of the heads are tilted downwards so they must be looking at somebody who is dead or resting, down in the ditch there.

'T-boned,' father man says.

We could stop. Other people have stopped. A woman with very white legs is holding a first-aid kit in a plastic lunch box in her hand. People stop to be helpful. An ambulance could be on its way and a tow truck to clear the road. The police keep a broom in the back of their car for sweeping accident debris. We don't stop.

Father man takes his position again in the left-hand lane. He checks his mirrors, accelerates, moves up through the gears. Back on the road.

Λ

When you are a pedestrian you should always walk along the side of the road closest to the oncoming cars so they can see your eyes before they hit you. When your back is turned they will see your soft hair covering the soft part at the back of your soft head. Later they will see where the soft part of your soft head hits the bonnet. The bonnet will be dented like a warm pillow in the morning and your head will be resting on the road then.

There won't be a stain or a mark. Blood and tar are much the same.

∧

Here is a dog trotting down the highway with a green plastic bag of shopping in its mouth. There is something inside the bag, but I can't see what it is.

∧

When I walked up Struttle Road hill to tell the lady with the pink glasses that her Mazda was ready a white dog slunk around a gate with its lips pulled back. I didn't see it until we were nearly touching. It slouched out of the way with its big head low and heavy. My heart bunched up and clutched itself. The suddenness. A big white dog, right there in front of me. It might have been chance that the dog came through the gate just then. Maybe it hadn't even seen me. The dog turned and walked along the side of Struttle Road where I had just been walking. It was a dirty white dog. It wasn't a dog that people touch or that has a bowl and a collar. It was a dog with a chain hanging off it, a dog that will get a lump on its belly, that eats in the dirt and keeps its head down and shits behind a tree and tries not to be noticed, because while it knows it is a dog with its dog's body and dog's ways, it knows it is the wrong kind of dog. The dog didn't see me because it was seeing itself.

When a mother needs to go to the toilet a place has to be found with trees and bushes and everyone has to stay in the car and pretend it isn't happening. The mother walks in a long way through the bushes, placing her feet carefully between the clumps of grass in case of snakes. It takes a long time. Once, when my mother barely had her legs back in the car, father man drove off because he could see a caravan coming up behind.

^

There are birds that only fly the road. Plain, working birds that have their own stretch. Up and down the road they fly, through the trail of bitumen haze. Sometimes they do time with us, coasting in our slipstream. You have to be thankful for how they give the road a purpose, make the road a place. A circling hawk is never pitiful and the flock birds that cruise across the horizon are always going somewhere new.

^

A torn lizard, then some pieces of a rabbit. At a death and near a death there will be tyre stains, bloodstains and little lumps of ripped flesh furred on the top side only.

^

A sunburnt man on a bicycle wearing a singlet and white gardening gloves. If you put a glove on your hand it can be a comfort. It can be like having your hand held by another hand. Or at least I imagine so. Sometimes, when father man is out, I put my hand in the workshop vice. Just testing. I wind both plates so they are snug, then wind again until they crush and leave it for a count of fifty. One elephant, two elephants, fifty elephants. Fifty hippopotamuses would take longer but that word is chock-a-block with fun.

^

A yellow school bus sign smattered with black bullet holes. They must be doing a new topic at school by now. I've missed the old topic too. Every day I wake up and my heart pumps and my lungs breathe and my blood goes around. Knowing about the first settlers and the wool industry doesn't change anything, or the *Jabberwocky*, which they say is good, but it would be bad if we did it.

^

At speed, the road has a strong, hard wind. To be out of it, at the roadside stop, where the wind is soft and round, is unsettling. Because I am wearing shorts the wind feels like a hand reaching between my legs. Father man's hands are only for the road here, and I'm fine with that.

^

The mirror is too high on the wall at the roadhouse toilets. Open mouth. Shut mouth. A face. A cave. Check that the tongue is still padlocked inside the mouth. Good to take a minute off the road, though. If you keep on driving in other countries you get somewhere. You get to a new country. Perhaps you get to the sea? If you keep on driving in this country you can lay your whole life down on the road.

^

The television is on in the corner of the roadhouse cafe. We sit four in a line and eat our toasted sandwiches. It's a quiz show. The host grimaces and lifts his lips from his teeth. I know three answers but I don't say. Then it's the news. There's a report on Australian pedestrian injuries and deaths. The parts of the car causing injury were the front bumper bar, the leading edge of the bonnet, the front edge of the front mudguard and the upper surface of the bonnet. Some pedestrians that were hit did not look, or misjudged a gap in the traffic. Some claimed they looked. Some pedestrians that were hit stood in the centre of the road or deliberately ran into a vehicle. Some pedestrians that were hit were children that, for some reason, hesitated when crossing the road.

^

A big lady kangaroo tipped on one side. Her palomino fur full of evening sun, her black gloved paws clasped in greeting.

∧

These are my inventions: a false floor that fits behind the front seats of a car so one person can sleep on the back seat and one person can sleep on the floor without the hump in the middle cutting them in half. Tools for the kitchen to prevent boring tasks. A walk-in hot air drying cupboard next to the shower so there's no need for effort with towels. A death sound built into the road and triggered by a car travelling over it to keep innocent animals away.

∧

The last bit of driving, when the sun is down, is the saddest. The arms of the trees reaching out across the road. Animals line up behind the roadside fences to watch the darkening cars. There is no instrument that tells the driver when the headlights are required. One car flips its light switch and everyone follows. The road is a black strap under the beam of the headlights, then the softness of the gravel as we pull into the roadside stop. There are thousands of vehicles in circulation on the highway and many vehicles are stopped here. All night the sound of the car doors unsticking and punching shut again as people go off to the grass. Each sleeping car keeps its safe travelling distance. For a few seconds when a door is opened or a match is struck to light a cigarette you can see inside a car, but then the darkness takes it back again.

On my first night in the car I startled each time father man moved in his seat, but I'm used to it now. I could laugh at how safe I am down here with my brother spread out above me on the back seat like a shield. Twelve days ahead.

The cars wake and get on the road early the next morning. Toilet paper streamers wave us off from the roadside grass.

∧

A herd of raggy emus run through some bushes on the side of the road. They don't look at us. Their necks can only look front-ways.

∧

A dog on a box, a sheep on a stone, the black stump, the long paddock of the road. It isn't dishonourable if a town doesn't have an avenue of honour. Perhaps the trees were planted but didn't grow, or a fire burnt them down.

∧

There are no trees on the plain. Families live here without trees. The government should buy them some. Here is a flattened bird with its beak cracked against the bitumen. It was licking the road and got stuck by the tongue. This dead kangaroo has her legs open. Her pale underside feels shameful to look at, like the blank groin of a doll.

∧

People say there is nothing out here, in the outback. You won't find a shop, you won't find a house, you won't find a hairdresser, you won't find any cities, you won't find a hall that has a dancing class except it's cancelled as the teacher has gone away. You won't find comics, you won't find books, you won't find a painting in a frame, you won't find curtains, you won't find flowers, you won't find a lunch box and you won't find a hairbrush. Nowhere will you find a man with his trousers undone and a screwdriver in his hand. The nothing in the outback is thick and rich. If we stopped the car now and I opened my door and walked off the road and into the outback, I think the outback would kill me. Or maybe I would kill the outback. I think only one of us would survive.

∧

We pass a truck with a roll of road on its tray. I can't see what sort of road it is because the surface is on the inside in the same way jam is curled inside a Swiss roll. These are the different types of road that you can buy:

Blue road.

Purple road with black stains where potholes have been fixed. It's the same with silver fillings in teeth – dentists like their repairs to be noticed.

Light grey road with rough stones that are proud of the bitumen because the mixture was mixed wrong. This road is sticky and tiring for cars.

Pink road, but only in small sections so it's a surprise.

Black road that always looks dry.

Grey road with cat's eyes and white shoulder lines and white centre lines, sporty like a tennis court, and white posts every few breaths to announce to the land around, *this is the road, see, here is the road.*

Black road that darkens when wet.

Flecked grey road.

Smooth white road. This road is used just before a bridge to introduce the idea of water.

Orange gravel road. Gravel road doesn't come in a roll – it's poured onto the road through a sieve.

Roads stained by paints and acids.

Skid-marked roads where tyres have gripped and screamed, then fled.

Roads where one surface is in conflict with the others.

Roads with corroded edges like old ladies' lips.

Roads worried by junctions and intersections, where one road becomes another.

Roads that the land is taking back.

Roads scarred by procedures and operations.

Roads that are unsure of their form.

Roads over rivers and creeks and streams that cry out with the sound of what is flowing beneath them.

∧

Today, hardly anyone has spoken. Other families' cars can be full of words for the holidays. *Pink sky at night*, and *fifty cents for the first person to see the sea*, and *are we there yet?* which is a happy joke because they have somewhere good to go. Some families hold their breath over bridges so they'll never drown.

∧

We stretch and yawn. We mill around the car at the road-side stop. My mother says, 'oh, look at that stick, that's an unusual-looking stick.'

It's a trail of dog shit. There are fat sections and thin sections like the carriages of a toy train linked together with strands of grass. She bends down to pick it up.

^

My mother's scalp is greasy beneath her hair. Here's a fence creeping away between two hills. The road in evening gloom. Somebody planned all of this. Somebody wanted all of this to happen out here.

^

A flower farm with a white delivery truck parked in the driveway. The sign on the side of the truck says, *Everything's Coming Up Roses.*

When I have money I will send myself flowers with love words on a white card.

^

Lunch at the roadhouse cafe. Father man is using the toilet to shave so we can sit and read car and fishing magazines as we drink our apple juice.

What people want is transport with all the trimmings. What people want is a bench seat in mint green vinyl and four on the floor. What people want is a shelf under the glove box for maps and handbags and a mirror behind the shade visor for the female to redden her lips so the male who drives will be reminded of her sexual parts. What people want is for their father to be dead so the road is all for them and they can go wherever they want. But then, surprisingly, what people want is not the latest model car. What they want is the car their father wanted but wasn't smart enough and didn't have a good enough job to get. They want this car but with all the up-to-date features – a tape deck, automatic blinkers, a cigarette lighter. The car is sleek and fast and low. The car has potential. If only they could get around that one slow driver who's always in front, that slow driver in the heap-of-crap car, then everything in the world would belong to them.

That's according to an article about the car in modern times by a car psychologist from America.

There's a lot to worry about out in the world. One thing that's certain is that prices are rising and everything will soon be too expensive to buy.

^

A small trailer is a happy sight. When you tow a trailer you are always being followed; there's the live weight of it behind you, like a dog pulling on its lead. You can use it to measure things: a trailer load of sand, a trailer load of wood or chicken shit. There's no engine, no moving parts that need tending. And the look of it – small and square, sometimes covered, sometimes open, and the happy ball joint connected to the car with its stumpy tail.

^

Gaining, gaining, gaining – there's always someone coming up behind. But first a milk tanker to be overtaken – a silver cannon loaded with white.

^

It's nice to travel next to the powerlines, their pole shoulders straight across the sky, and to think about the tree each pole could have been. I saw a power pole lying down on the back of a very long truck with a rag tied around its end – a wooden hot dog. The road is happy to have the company of the poles and wires. The surface of the road dips and rises, dips and rises, to keep time with the slack black strings. One burnt power pole has been left standing high up the hill, all ready for the crucifixion.

^

Father man controls the engine's breathing with the throttle and the choke. Father man controls the steering and the placement of the vehicle on the road.

The car kills insects with wings (moths, dragonflies, lacewings, mosquitos, butterflies, flies) and the other insects that come with them – bugs and spiders. The car kills most sorts of birds although the emu we drove over was already dead. The car kills rabbits, bandicoots, hopping mice, numbats, skinks, rats, lizards, wombats, snakes, echidnas, goannas, wallabies and kangaroos. The car kills a bat and an eagle. The eagle had a choice between picking at the innards of a rabbit, and life. It chose the innards of the rabbit, and death. Each kill is a road accident – and just like when we saw the red car and the green car, we don't stop. We kill a fox and on the outskirts of the town of Cobar we kill a ginger cat with a low-hanging stomach and half a tail.

The insects and small birds get sucked into the orbit of the Holden as it cuts its car-hole out of the wind, but surely anything larger has a choice?

∧

Driving into a dark sky. Soon rain will fall.

What is best to fall on you – a tonne of feathers or a tonne of hammers? Have you seen a hammer fly? The wood, the head, the wood, the head, the shiny rabbit ears rotating through the air... But it's a trick. Feathers have more volume than hammers so they displace more air. I'd still choose the hammers. The slam, the bruise, the blood. Family life. The press of the feathers would be too soft to bear.

∧

A country town can have a guard of trees announcing it – English-shaped trees in a polite queue to trick you into thinking that you could be arriving somewhere good. At the petrol station at Cunnamulla I'm bleeding. Well, I'm not quite bleeding yet. First the brown smear, then the red fall. Mornings are tricky at the roadside stop. The first time I stand up I have to hope the pad hasn't moved and there isn't a leak.

∧

Father man hates the caravans that beetle along in front of us. The women that belong to caravan men are heavy about the shoulders, reinforced for towing.

∧

A hawk polices overhead. Out the side window: strips of torn tyre rubber from where it has escaped its wheel and gotten free. A black stain where the rubber has burnt the road.

∧

Speed and sway. A shock absorber can check rapid movement. The only thing that could stop us now is a collision with a road train, or a wall.

∧

Our circling tyres are a joke to the road. It has already been rolled. Ordinary cars, not road trains, are only the slightest rub on its surface, a mere tickle.

Driving over a bridge. The dead road hard beneath us, then a rise, a buoyancy, as the tyres sense another family of air beneath them. They tighten, harden, bounce. Where would we go if we could get free of the road?

^

Dabs of insect blood on the windscreen. The speed of impact milks them dead.

^

Hours and hours of the plains. Thick white sky presses against the road. No fences, no edges, just flatness. A darker moustache where the sky meets the scrub. If you could drive over to that place, to the horizon, you'd drive right off the world. The grey road turns to ice in front of us but always dries as we race to meet it. Trucks in the distance elongate, skate, then firm. Night falling to meet the last of the day. The dusk trembles – is it sexy? As it gets darker our headlights joust with oncoming vehicles; their high beams cross and drill us, find the white plates of our faces.

^

You can't force an engine seal. You have to check that each edge is seated snugly against the other. Sometimes father man has to leave the car at night because of the congestion. He'll moan and adjust his trousers and open the car door and walk off, gingerly, into the night. No one will stir. My mother breathes her night breaths. My brother breathes his night breaths. I pretend I don't know that father man is gone. Time is grainy for a while. I can pretend there is nothing that I know.

^

On the side of the road tiny bullet flies dart at our wetnesses: eyes, nostrils, lips, first of the day's sweat. A string could be a snake. A tear could be a lake. Out here we are the beginning and the end of everything.

^

Skittery tumbleweeds rush across the road in front of us. All afternoon low grey bushes wave at us as we pass. It's not because of us; it's just the weather of the road.

^

A petal-eared rabbit asleep on the edge of the hard shoulder, the white line for its pillow.

^

The news is on television in the roadhouse. Somewhere in this country there's a bushfire in the hills. Houses are burning and a shed is collapsing and a helicopter has taken some blurry footage of the sweet white smoke from the air. It's interesting to see. It isn't made up. The four of us sit in front of our lunch and watch it together. The chief fireman is interviewed. He is bald with silver badges on his shirt and a fat wedding ring and a heavy identity bracelet that slops around on his wrist as he points and gestures. The bushfire is serious but he's enjoying himself and we are too. When the bushfire story is finished it's back to the cricket. My mother pats her mouth with her serviette and sighs the proper sigh for a natural disaster and we look down at our smeared plates again. A cyclone would be good now, or an earthquake – any catastrophe brought on by mother nature to take us out of ourselves.

∧

The uncoupled trailer of a road train abandoned at our roadside stop. Its cab has gone on ahead to hunt. Every so often a spaghetti-legged man riding a bicycle with pain around his mouth.

∧

At Barcaldine my mother gives me money to buy more pads. I don't know how much blood is the right amount.

The woman at the check-out in the supermarket takes the pads over to the service counter where she wraps them up in a sheet of newspaper and sticky-tapes the end down before she puts them in the bag.

^

A road dream. A tyre stain on the road like the brackets around a sentence starts to writhe because it is a snake. The snake bites its tail to make a wheel and races the car. I put my hand out of the window to touch the snake-wheel as it passes but its skin is burning hot from the friction of the road. Faster, faster we go, the car and the snake.

^

The river trees are rusting from the river water. The river stain creeps up their trunks in the same way that rust creeps up the car's panels behind the paint. Sometimes a rusted car will be lying on its roof in a paddock and father man will say, 'look at that Jap crap.'

^

There's a galah for sale on the edge of this town and puppies in the next. A sign for ferrets going cheap in faded red paint on corrugated iron. You won't find an animal for sale in a town or right out in the bush. It's only on the edge of town where they have too many and would rather have the money. If it's your birthday your mother might tell the father man to take the rutted driveway next to the sign and then she'll get her purse from her bag and walk into one of the sheds near the house and come out with a box with a squirmy kitten in it and stab marks in the cardboard made with scissors so the kitten has air. The people who owned the kitten won't come out to wave goodbye because they are so sad to see it go.

^

The road is in our teeth, in the fat of our buttocks, the skin on the backs of our legs, our spines, the soles of our feet. When we stop the land is there, sideways, fanning out, opening up along each side of the road, but it isn't where we're going. We walk the white line behind the car to stretch our legs. Over a week of driving now. We don't leave the road. The press of the car against our flesh. That's all we need.

^

The yellow paddocks are beautiful when the cubes of hay have been left sitting in their regular pattern on the land. They could be houses on a new estate or items in a super-market for the sheep to browse and buy. *Just browsing* is what you say when you don't have any money but you want to touch things and see their colours as if you do.

Nobody knows what you have in your pocket. Most children are poor, but not everyone has nothing.

^

My mother doesn't get to drive much, not that I care about that. Father man looks stupid sitting in the passenger's seat, his hands slack in his lap. When it's time for them to swap places my mother walks around the back of the car, past the boot, to take her new seat. Father man walks around the front, past the engine. It's a changing of the guard, but there's never any danger that they might meet.

^

As we drive I can see where the air sits on top of the hills. There's a slice of air that isn't as blue. It's a place you could live up there – in a hut maybe or a cave – and the sky would let you in. There would be air enough to go around.

^

Up ahead a two-lane flared intersection, then a large roundabout for cars to circle in pairs. A yellow Cortina is curving in alongside us. It's coming in fast, the Cortina – it's really flying. It reaches us and holds our speed so we swing around the island of the roundabout together. Father man isn't sure of the exit. He jerks his head about in exasperation. My mother is holding the map of Australia out in front of her. She shakes it as if rattling the paper will soothe father man and prevent, or cover, his anger.

Through my window I can see inside the yellow Cortina. There is just the one person, a young woman, driving and opening her mouth wide and pink to sing along with the car radio. I can see her hands on the steering wheel, which she holds very gently in the way people do when they are balancing a fancy cake on a plate. As the Cortina pulls ahead slightly I can see right across the empty back seat of her car and through the far window to a dusty hedge that borders the traffic island in the middle of the roundabout. The sunlight through the car windows paints an image of the two cars across the hedge. The Cortina is racing ahead of us now and the hedge image stretches then dissolves. I can see the back of the young woman's head getting smaller and smaller as she drives away, her dark hair swaying as she sings. I am happy for her. Perhaps I love her? Perhaps she can tell me what happens next?

∧

Above us is a cloud that has burst. An aeroplane has pierced the cloud and the white has come out in two lines behind its engines. Sad for the sky, but nobody cares about this.

∧

The best is when you are driving and a plane is flying over-head. Especially if it's flying low and in the same direction (this can happen near an airport). Even better would be the car and the plane and, on tracks next to the road, a train. (Or the train might be running beneath the road on an underground track but you can feel its rumble.) Imagine it – even if it's only for a moment, there are three engines making time together. The car, the plane, the train, pulling us away, taking us away to someplace new.

∧

Pain on the side of the road again. Pain with feathers. Pain with fur. Pain with scales.

∧

Piles of timber poles waiting in the railway yard with the bark hanging off them like tattered trousers. Good for an accidental fire. I wonder how much kindling it would take to get it all blazing.

When a boy scout rubs two sticks together to make fire the amount of work (elbow grease) he puts in is directly equivalent to the heat produced in the sticks. The mechanical equivalent of heat: the thermal equivalent of work. So the boy scout isn't needed, really. A machine could hold the sticks and thrust them against each other to create friction. Except that it's nice to imagine the boy in his shorts with his badges and his woggle and his hat, the boy with his fishing rod and his slingshot and his thick yellow hair falling over his eyes. There are lots of ways for men and boys to dress up and play their parts. Girls get to play parts too, but their costumes are not for science or the skills of life; they are for men to put their eyes on.

^

In America you can drive your car into restaurants and burger joints and a girl will come out in a purple skirt on rollerskates and take your order in her cardboard hat. In America big fat grown-ups drive their cars around like babies in prams. A soft burger to tear at with your hard teeth, a bottle of fizz with a straw for suckling. You can drive right into a bank. You can drive through the middle of a pet food store and they'll put your kitty litter in the boot.

Here's a drive-in movie theatre – a paddock recomissioned, now a car park forested with speaker poles and empty boxes of Maltesers being kicked around in the wind.

^

The road is pitted and greasy. The road is held in by kerb now. A sign for a smash repairer on the side of the bus stop. Light farm fencing gets darker and heavier, becomes town fencing, although now there's only humans and dogs to be kept in. Iron-roofed houses, tile-roofed houses clotted up together behind the tall paling fences. Side streets. A high school with chip bags sprouting from its chain-mesh fence.

The road is a highway now, except that it's slow and lined on either side with businesses nobody wants to go to. Sheet metal engineers, cheap conveyancing, electrical repairs, Quality Plumbing with Pride, ute specialists, Frank's Motorcycles and Spares, cabinet-makers, aquarium supplies, blinds and awnings, Peace of Mind Security Professionals, pumps, pool supplies, real estate, car rentals, feminine hygiene systems, water features and outdoor furniture, locksmiths, roofing and guttering, marine supplies, trailers, panelbeaters, tyres and lube, air conditioning specialists. Each of these is in a box lining the road. Some of the boxes with glass fronts and showrooms have reception areas; some have a roller door. Free parking on premises, at rear.

A car in front of us, a car behind. New and used cash registers. Blinds and canopies. Mobil fuel with car wash. Dave's Windscreens. A stream of cars flow in the other direction. Traffic lights now. Parked cars nose to tail. Streetlights. Commercial cookery supplies. Parking meters. Rubbish bins.

'It's a fucking nightmare,' father man says, as if it wasn't his idea, as if we have forced him here.

A fish and chip shop, a Chinese restaurant, a chemist

with sunhats on a stand outside. Cars flow and glide down the channel in front of the banked shops. Everyone is on their way.

An incline. Many of the brown pavers that make up the footpath have lifted and dirty yellow sand is coming through. Father man's window is down and the smell of petrol and sunscreen and exhaust fans from the takeaway shops and the salt-saturated filmy air is streaming in.

And here, oh, the road is ending. We can't go any further. This is the other side of the country. What we've been driving through is human life thickening up before it runs out of land.

There's a car park. In front of the car park is a strip of pale sand and in front of that the large, loose sea.

HOME AGAIN

While we have been away, the fat lady has bought a car. There's something wrong with it already so she has parked it in front of the workshop for father man to notice once he gets home. The fat lady's car is just a run-around. It's a forest green Mini. As soon as I see it I know that I'm going to drive it on the highway at night and I know that I am going to hurt it.

My mother walks around the house calling for Babette and then she searches under the beds and looks in all of the cupboards. My brother and I don't help. Babette won't be coming home – if there was somewhere else to go why would you come back here?

It rains on the first night that we are home and the rain is kind. I don't want to go out in it. I would like to stay in my bed – the mattress is long and flat with no transmission hump pushing up against me. My mother goes to her room early. How eager we are to close our doors on each other.

My door, I know, will be opened. Because of the trip there's a gap and time must be made up for. Because of the trip father man experienced losses and now it's time to pay. It is urgent like I've seen a dog is, or a horse or a bull.

Afterwards I climb out of the window and walk to the tip in the rain. I like how the raindrops hold on to my hair before they drip away. The early settlers thought that rain would follow the plough, but rain takes no notice of people. It's just a coincidence that I like to go out walking in the rain and that the drumming of the rain on the roof covered the sounds that father man made.

The feathers that came out of the rip in my pillow are not real feathers. They are man-made sanitised fibre. They are made in China. When I cleaned myself up, when I got dressed for my walk, I put a handful of the white feathers in the pocket of my jeans. The rain held back to let me into the night. Father man, my mother and my brother were asleep in their beds. The yawn of a bonnet didn't wake them. I patted the radiator of the Holden, with some affection, I think. I could have taken a spanner and removed a part – perhaps the starter motor? I could have taken the part behind the workshop or onto the lawn and buried it with the others, but instead I took the feathers from my pocket, unstuck them with my fingers and placed them on the hard surface of the rocker cover, one by one. Most will scatter as soon as father man opens the bonnet. A few might remain. A demonstration of soft.

It's good that I don't go to school the next day because the Avon lady comes. Cicadas are doing their practice in the damp air. Leaves are dead on the ground. A brown Torana drives up. A lady sits in the car filling in a form and then she drags the handbrake on and gets out. She has her pink lipstick around her mouth and she has her white plastic court shoes and a gold chain tight around her ankle. She looks at the house and then at the workshop. She must have heard the cricket on the radio because she picks her basket up off the back seat of the Torana and walks through the gravel and the pine needles towards the workshop. She doesn't lift her feet high enough to account for the slope of the ramp so her high heels scrape on the concrete. If the Avon lady knew the first thing about cars she would have known that the workshop was built high up because there is a pit shaped like a coffin in the middle of it, but dug into the ground at the same height as a man so he can stand underneath the cars and work on them with his tools scattered around the opening and with a light.

The Avon lady walks in through the roller door. I don't follow. I'm behind the kerosene drum under the trees. I don't know what happens next. The concrete apron of the workshop is white in the sun and you can't see past the frame of the roller door into the darkness inside.

The Avon lady would have blinked a few times to adjust her eyes to the darkness. She would have taken her catalogue out of her plastic basket and perhaps put it down on the workbench, or perhaps even put it into his hand. It goes to show that not everyone can see what he has. If she got close to him she would have felt what he has pressing against her stomach where her blouse was tucked into her pleated skirt – blue nylon – knife pleats or ray pleats? I'm never sure, but every bit of it was pleated, except at the back where she'd been sitting on it, so around her bum it was flattened like the lid of a cardboard box.

She isn't in the workshop for long. When she comes out she doesn't look different. Nothing is my fault. She walks back down the ramp and gets into her car.

I want her to see me, to smile at me. I want to ask her about the terry towelling seat covers in the Torana. Are they the ones that tie on underneath or are they fitted with elastic? I want the chain on her ankle and her root perm and everything in the Avon autumn catalogue except the wooden toys and the butterdish shaped like a cow. I want the Avon lady to stay here and live with us, or better still to open the passenger door of her car and move the boxes of catalogues out of the way so we can all get into the back together – so the Avon lady can rescue us, the three of us, my mother, my brother, myself, and take us far away.

Sunday. The garden string is sad. It is coiled around itself green and hard. My mother is driving; my brother is tossing the string up and down in his hand as we drive back up the highway from the nursery. The three of us can go on an outing together now that we are home. My brother's window is open and when I look across I can see the ball of string held in the frame of the window for a second like it is a painting. The green string is in the foreground of the painting; the scene outside the window, the dirty roadside bush, is the background. The string could easily go out the window if my brother fumbles, but nobody says this. My mother's plants died while we were away so we went on an outing to the nursery. She didn't buy more plants but she bought the string.

My mother parks the Holden under the shade of the pine trees, facing the house. She pulls on the handbrake and takes the key from the ignition. My brother's hand is still opening and closing around the string. We watch the brown house in front of us. The paint is called mission brown. If we forget the house is made of wood the paint will remind us. The lawn around the house is yellow but it is still quite nice at night, high and mattressy on its runners. My brother has stopped throwing the string now. His hand is on the doorhandle, but he doesn't open it. He is waiting for our mother to open her door and get out of the car. She could always change her mind. Maybe there is someplace else for us to go?

Our mother is looking through the windscreen at the house in the same bored way as if she is still driving. It is how she looks at the television. I watch the petrol gauge as it sinks its spider's leg below the horizon. Our mother has a red spotted headscarf over her hair. She has her gold-framed glasses on. She isn't bothering with her contact lenses today – she's giving her eyes a rest. The three of us sit in the car together, watching the house.

I close my eyes and lift the bonnet. I remove the timing case and chain tensioner. I remove the bolt, lock washer and plain washer securing the camshaft timing wheel. When you put your mind in the engine some of what your body is saying – about being too hot, wanting a drink, needing to cry – can be turned down for a while. The manual can be relied upon. It is the same each time you open it. The same parts, the same hands. One exploded view sits next to another. No breath. No noise. No lies. How is it that paper can be separate from time? How is it that outside the world of paper something is always happening next?

My mother opens her door and gets out of the car and we go inside. Not the string though – the string sits bunched up in its green ball on top of the beer fridge by the back door. When father man opens the fridge after dinner the ball of string bounces down in front of his face and he swears at it. Because he is a man he must catch it, even though there is a risk he might spill his beer.

Two days of rain. Water pooled on the road. I am going to the dentist with my mother. The car lunges through old spray. We don't put our eyes on each other – there's no need. Each morning you get back up on your legs and you don't think about anything at all, except breakfast.

My mother has lipstick on and a red t-shirt with flowers on the chest. She reads *Family Circle* in the waiting room as the dentist puts the tools in my mouth. No chance to speak. When the dentist drills the top off my infected tooth his nostrils flare. I am not the only one in the world that is rotten; he must have smelled it before.

Later, the fat lady has gone shopping so I watch *Get Smart* on the television in her living room. The best bit is the beginning with Maxwell Smart in his little red car and then all of the doors opening and closing behind him as he goes down underground into the secret vault where the good spies work. The *Get Smart* music is my favourite music in the world.

During the ads I play with Babette and look at the fat lady's things. She has a new set of steak knives in a box – wooden handles, copper screws, jagged edges. They won't match her forks but it doesn't matter with meat.

The next show is about an American family. The father with the beard, the mother with the perm, the son with a crew cut because he's in the cadets, the daughter with a golden ponytail pulled high and tight. They eat pancakes together at a shiny table. The boy wants to borrow the family car to take a girl out on a date, but he doesn't want to say that so he makes up an unbelievable story. Each member of the family takes a turn saying a line. After they say their line they wait for the laughing-in-a-can to come up around them and then to die down again. This is normal for an American family – not just that they are happy, but that all the invisible laughers around them are happy too.

Tonight for dinner it's fish fingers, red jelly and ice cream. My mother has a lot of trouble cooking the fish fingers and keeping the crumbs on them. Father man doesn't have dessert, he has another green can, and then he dead-locks the doors.

My mother's preparations for the night take a long time. She puts on the radio. She has a hot shower. She shaves her legs. She dries herself with a pink towel and applies powders to her body. Then she sits at her dressing table on a spindly chair with curved metal legs, to tweeze her eyebrows and lotion her face and neck. When you are getting a vehicle ready for storage it's advisable to top off the petrol and the battery and lubricate the doors. My mother must concentrate on her female procedures; she is in her own world now, not reachable, not to be disturbed.

Two bites on my jaw that I scratch into one. Blood on my pillowcase sticks the nylon to my face in the night. When I sit up in the morning the pillow comes with me. The more I rear back from it, the more it comes.

Out of the window I can see two planes in the sky – they know how to keep their distance. The sky clicks with heat, clear turquoise brought to the front, and every morning swarms of insects rising from the lawn. Father man must have seen the blood on my face. He might have closed his eyes, but he didn't turn his head away.

∧

Back to work in the workshop, in the afternoon. Father man tells me to hold the spanner firm. His head is close to mine. Wax is fruiting around the hair stalks in his ear. The spanner slips. The head of it chimes against the clutch plate. I shut my eyes so my fingers can work faster, finding the bolt, tickling it free. It is a habit, a skill, I have learnt from working in the dark. I don't know I've done it until I open my eyes again and father man is looking at my face. His mouth hangs slack for a second and then he shuts it. Does he know something? Do I care if he knows something?

This is where television is good for learning how to hold the pieces of your face in one expression that could be happy or could be sad, but has nothing real behind it. It's a Thursday. I don't know what other families are doing, but I know they aren't doing this.

Later, on *Hogan's Heroes*, the prisoners decide to sabotage a convoy of German supply trucks on their way to the front line. Schultz is guarding the trucks while the drivers have dinner at Stalag 13. Schultz is an oaf and it doesn't take much for the prisoners to get him into conversation and offer him their home-brewed liquor and get him drunk. The prisoners load the drunken Schultz onto the back of one of the trucks where he snores happily, then they use hacksaws to cut part way through the engine hoses in the German supply trucks. The plan is for the trucks to be some distance away from Stalag 13 before they break down. This is so the sabotage can't be linked to them.

These are the different types of sabotage:

An act of sabotage through the loosening of essential connections.

An act of sabotage in which false connections are made.

An act of sabotage by cutting.

An act of sabotage through removal.
Removal followed with burial.

An act of electrical sabotage.
Electrical damage is quick and clinical. Perhaps it is female? Tracks can easily be covered with a fire in the circuitry. Scorched electrics have the pleasant smell of burnt toast. It's a family-friendly smell with overtones of the kitchen and winter mornings and everyone snug indoors.

An act of sabotage through drainage.
This is best when the oil is clean. When the oil is fresh and new it will run fast like golden syrup and be soaked up by the gravel overnight, leaving very little trace.

An act of sabotage involving swallowing.
Some of the screws for Japanese appliances – a transistor radio, for example – are so small they

are easier than peanuts to pass down the throat.
The Japanese screws can't be replaced so the lid
of the transistor radio's battery compartment will
always be loose then, causing poor connection
and interruption at important times, like during
the cricket.

An act of sabotage where you go for the heart
of the car.

An act of sabotage where you pick at the edges.
There are many ways for a machine to come
undone. Also, avoid using the hacksaw; its teeth
are hell to clean.

The manual for the Holden is under my bed again. In *Exploded View of Front Wheel Hub and Drum Assembly* there is the large dark circle of the hub. Transiting behind it are the grease-retaining inner seal, the inner bearing and the tiny hub bolt. Transiting in front of it are the bearing cover, the castellated nut, the sub axle washer, the outer bearing, the wheel hub nut and the very, very tiny drum attaching bolt. The creamy paper around each part is the galaxy of the hub and drum assembly. This could be the whole world – yes? All of the circular parts orbiting around one another and never touching or getting hurt and always being happy?

The next night it's just me in my bed, but after a

while I get up anyway. I rip one of the index pages from the manual and fold it over and over like we learnt at school, making a simple fan. I climb out of my window and skip across the grass. I feed the paper fan through the radiator cap of father man's Holden. The manual for the engine and the actual engine can be together now, with nobody getting in between.

A car is always better than the bus. Where am I going today? Nowhere that matters. The bus finally comes in its coat of white exhaust fumes and shrieks its painful shriek as it gears down to stop for me. The driver moves his neck but no parts of his face as he takes my coins. He has a red am/fm transistor radio between his thighs. The old people put their eyes on me as I walk down the aisle, then put them back on the windows. Nobody beautiful has ever caught a bus. The seat has a stain but it is never in the exact place it would be if the stain had come out of you. The road churns past beneath us.

Sharon gets on the bus further down the hill. She comes and sits next to me. I have a shell for her that I found on the beach. It's in the bottom of my bag and I think about giving it to her. Sharon tells me about her tyre boy again. I don't say about my time with the tyre boy at the Best Western motel because it was only made up. It only happened in my mind.

Looking out of the window of the bus I can see pieces of a car accident left behind on the side of the road, but without the cars. It's like a paddock where the animals are gone but strings of wool and shit remain, marking the places where they stood in the grass. Pieces of a car accident on the road can look like the stuff that's been emptied out of a handbag or a purse. It isn't money; it isn't anything useful at all. It's yours though, so you carry it around with you anyway.

The bus slows down as we go past the arrester bed. The bus slows again, then stops, groaning on the hill, because a tow truck is dragging a semitrailer out of the arrester bed in front of us. Even Sharon stands up to look. The semitrailer has white tarpaulins roped down over its load. It doesn't look happy at being dragged out of the cage of gravel. The orange gravel is pouring, sleeting off it, as it comes unstuck. The tow truck tugs and finally the semi breaks free, a shower of gravel pinging off the cab like hailstones. A soft orange cloud balloons into the air above the truck as if it has done a colourful burp. The bus gets going then, picks up speed and continues down the hill. I go back to my seat. Sharon has gotten out some Minties but she doesn't offer them.

Sharon is bad at stealing, but my hands were made for taking. My mouth was made for lies. The thing is only stolen when you bring it across that first time. As soon as

154

it's in your pocket, or even in your bag, it's yours.

I steal a penknife for me, and one for Sharon, from the camping store. Sharon is going to give it to the tyre boy at the automotive because they've been going for a month now. It's an anniversary present. She won't say where she got the penknife from and I don't think he'll ask. He'll just take it as his due.

A Holden panel van comes in. We don't get many panel vans in up here. The panel van is black but without the painted flames licking the sides that I've seen in magazines. They mainly belong to boys that surf. I don't know why the panel van has been brought to father man's workshop here, where it's hot and dry and far away from the sea.

It's a full moon the first night the panel van is in. I brush my hair and smear vaseline on my lips. The metal door of the panel van squeals as it comes free. What happens in the factory the first time a new door is opened? Is there a ceremony? Do the factory men stand around and watch? First there was a sheet of metal, then there was a cut, now there is a door. The door is pulled free, leaving the metal around it behind – an offcut, a discard – or perhaps, like pastry, the metal can be mashed up and reshaped to make another door?

I climb into the panel van and lie down on the chipboard floor. There are no windows, just gilled vents along the sides. It's the same model as they have on *Matlock Police* for the paddy wagons. Why are the police so careful to protect the heads of the criminals as they put them in the back of the paddy wagon when everyone knows they kick them and punch them down at the station? I wish there was a mattress in here. You could fit more than two people lying side by side. Human volume: the sack of you, the sack of me. I put my candle stub in the ashtray and light it with the lighter from the pocket of my jeans. The flame dips and sputters then glows golden against the metal. I trace the outline of the Holden lion stamped on the ashtray with my fingers. The lion is sitting proudly on its haunches, the boulder resting beneath its paw. This is where it all began – men watching a lion rolling a stone.

Here I am, here I am, ready for you, in the panel van. I say a page I have remembered from *Seven Little Australians* and a little of the *Jabberwocky*. I have on my Amco jeans and the underpants I stole from the changing room at the pool. There might be traces of the other girl on them, but it's probably a good thing and I can't ever put them in the wash. I have on my western shirt with the pearly press-studs so it won't be hard to get at me when you come. I blow out the candle and lie down on the floor of the panel van. I close my eyes. I say some songs slowly so they sound like prayers. I try to sleep a while.

I think I was waiting for the tyre boy from the automotive. Only I didn't tell him that I was waiting for him, and he didn't know that I was there.

Let me explain about smiling. You don't just open your mouth: you pull it back and show your yellow teeth. The lips are pink or red. A smile will be the thing he'll like best about you.

Some days there can be touching that doesn't make a mark: a haircut, an injection, the dentist. You make it happen when you put your skin in the way of someone else. I stab a drawing-pin into my palm so I can ask my mother to dig it out.

Here is a chance to talk – my mother dabbing at the bottle of Mercurochrome with a tissue from her red handbag. A child learns speech because a mother speaks to it. A mother starts talking to you in the womb. She might even play old-fashioned music that doesn't have singing. A father won't speak to something he can't see. After you are born it will annoy a father to lean down so he can catch the high soft spit language that comes from your small girl's mouth. For a man, a boy's voice is in a better register; it's always easier to hear.

My mother sticks a bandaid across my palm. The skin is still wet so it won't stay on for long. 'Stupid girl,' she says. 'Don't do it again.'

Perhaps I should go back to sounds? S is for snake. R is for rip. It's one thing to make the sounds that form a word – not much effort at all, it barely takes thought. But the weight of the word on the person receiving it, the struggle with it, forever pulling a braked truck uphill…

The next morning a flock of parrots shriek in the pine trees outside the workshop. Twentee-eight, twentee-eight. A circus. They are unnatural colours. Their beaks are open, their pink cockled tongues shamelessly on display.

The fat lady comes over to the fence and calls out. A pigeon is trapped in her toilet. Fifty cents to catch it. I use the green towelling mat with two arms that hugs the toilet bowl. I lay the mat on the air above the bird and let it take them both down to the lino. The fat lady waits outside. I hold the bird and the mat under my arm and count for a few minutes to make it seem longer, like it is worth the money. Dead flies in the plastic light fitting, a matchbox on the cistern, dust on the skirting boards. The bird twitches in my armpit. Outside, when I throw the bundle into the air, the pigeon's claw is hooked in the towelling of the toilet mat, so this time the bird takes the mat down to the dirt on the fat lady's driveway before it struggles back into the air.

My brother's old Lee jeans have a coin pocket on the hip because men don't carry handbags or purses. I can feel the fifty cents pressing into me as I bend over and climb back through the fence, even though it isn't there. The fat lady said the mat was damaged. She said I didn't earn the fee.

Some nights I know I have been asleep – time has passed – but I come back without a dream. The bed is still and flat and I like how the pillow presses into my neck and how the inside of one leg fits snugly against the other. I don't understand where I've been – somewhere like death? It would be good to go there now.

I think I could live in the fat lady's laundry. I wouldn't need to throw anything out, just move a few things around to make space for a bed. I don't need a cupboard. Pyjamas under the pillow, clothes in a cardboard box. I can be out walking or up at the tip in the daytime – I'd only need to come in at night. The louvres are no barrier; it's easy to slide the glass from their metal trays. But what if the fat lady found me still asleep in the morning? Would she touch my hair or would she scream?

Father man has been oiling the rocker cover nuts and studs on the fat lady's Mini. The nuts are laid out like silver jubes on the workshop bench. I put three of them in my pocket and take them for a night-walk to the tip.

The white wires of the fences are tight where they are threaded through the posts then slack between them. Where do the birds go; where does the sun go? How can it be so warm still if the sun is no longer in the sky? Is the night a black felt blanket and every piece of the day still intact, just hidden behind it? The bitumen feels springy beneath my sandals, as if I'm walking on the top of a crusty loaf, or maybe I'm walking along the draped edge of the blanket. Is it just dark for us – for our family – and light for everyone else in the world?

Up Davidsons Road. The tip smells of sick that's cooled after being out in the sun. There are houses on one side of the road and bush on the other. No lights inside the houses. The windscreens of the cars parked in the driveways are the grey of television when it has been switched off. The cars wait outside the houses like chained dogs. When someone gets behind the wheel, the glass of the windscreen will clear again and the cars will give themselves over to being driven. Sometimes there is a rustle in the holly banksia. A goanna maybe? Nothing with fur could live here.

Hexagonal. The nuts are warm in my hand. I'm going home now. One at a time I flick the nuts into the bush.

Why am I myself? Should I be sorry about it?

∧

My brother has a swollen ear because a boy at the bus stop hit him. Our mother says, 'there's never a dull moment,' but she knows it isn't true.

Later, here is my brother in the kitchen with his hand inside our mother's handbag. It doesn't look comfortable. He's trying to get her purse out without fully undoing the top zip. He has to stand close to the edge of the table and paddle his hand in from above. It's safe because our mother is having a headache. Nobody ever has to tell us to be quiet.

Darren's been again. The Valiant has thick tyres that leave ugly marks in the gravel. A tyre can't make choices. Rolling isn't freedom when there's a chassis attached. The rear tyres punch and deepen the pattern made by the tyres in front. A blind person could read the tracks with their fingertips. If the blind person could speak they would say the tracks meant danger.

When you take a car out at night all of the owner's belongings go along with you – money, lipstick, food, tissues, pills, letters, cutlery, tools, maps, condoms, reading glasses on a chain, stickers for beer and teams and God. Sometimes a sweat stain on the back of the headrest. I don't like to night-drive a car that has a baby seat. I don't like to drive a car with toys.

It feels good to sit inside the fat lady's Mini in the

dark. A protected feeling. When you're a child they say, *look how you've grown*, but only while you are going upwards. As soon as you start going outwards nobody says anything. Their eyes get caught on the new flesh of you and then they look away. Any engine can be stripped down and reassembled if you know how. When a human body is taken apart there's no way it can ever be put back together again.

No parcel on the parcel shelf for me tonight, nothing in the glove box. I've never had gloves. Wickedness on television is a German with black leather hands.

As I drive away from the fat lady's house I apologise to the road beneath. It is insulting to drive so fast, so casually, over a road that knows the heat and weight of your feet on its back. It's not the same on distant, unfamiliar roads. Someone else walks those roads. They are not mine to care about.

Take off the handbrake at the highway, release the shuddery clutch. How pleasant to be out on a night like this. No headlights flattening out the road. Just the warm green light of the ignition switch and the glow from the rear-vision mirror as a truck comes up, as a truck gains on the Mini from behind. I write a letter to my brother in my mind – an explanation, just in case. But the little car is determined. We make it home again, despite the missing parts.

∧

My mother is having a tidy-up. This is what mothers do. They clean up the past so there's neatness and cleanness, so there's space for the future. My mother is throwing away a box of our childhood things, things from the time before. My brother drew cars when he was small. He drew rectangles balancing on puffy doughnut wheels. No hint of an engine. Always a spoked yellow sun in the sky. Off the paper, the hardness of the armature is so unexpected. How metal clenches. How the panels want to grip each other so a bonnet must be wrenched open, a door yanked from its hinges.

In my childhood drawing four horses are frolicking in a field. There's a black stallion with a curved neck and red nostrils and a golden palomino with a ribbon in her mane. A lean grey colt jumps a fallen tree, and a small brown pony has her head down in a tumble of hay. I have given up on colouring in the pony, or perhaps I ran out of brown before she was finished.

The fat lady's cat, our old cat, has kittens. My mother says it isn't possible because Babette was fixed but the fat lady says it can still happen. The fat lady gives my mother the kittens in a tea towel. The ones that are still alive don't look like kittens; they look like sausage rolls that have been sat on. Father man puts the kittens in a plastic shopping bag and drowns them in a bucket.

He should have put a rock or a brick in with them, because the bag still has air in it and the kittens thrash around and scratch him with their tiny claws as he pushes the different bits of the bag under the water with his hands.

Funny to think of the bag of kittens buried close to the car parts. I don't have to worry about what father man might dig up, because he gives me the wet plastic bag heavy with the sodden bodies of the kittens, and the shovel, and tells me to do the deed.

When I come back to the house to wash my hands afterwards father man is cracking the tab on his green can. Is there a latch in his throat that he unfastens to pour the yellow beer down? Not easy to imagine that his mouth was ever full of milk.

In *Photograph Showing Removal of Front Disc Brake Pads* both of my man's hands are held together, nearly touching at the fingertips, as they gently grip the shim. The manual shows that sometimes a delicate touch is needed to manipulate small parts. There's no physical reason why hands that work an engine can't do soft tasks – plaiting a girl's hair, icing a sponge cake, patting a baby's back to make it burp. Engine hands must be strong, but they don't have to be cruel. Cruelty happens outside of the manual. A large person never hurts a larger person. A large person will hurt a smaller person, or an animal, because it is permitted for them to do so.

The best thing, now, would be for the pop truck to come up the driveway. They know your order because you phone it in ahead each month. It doesn't stop you putting in a special order, if it's someone's birthday, for instance. The pop truck is a rigid-body flatbed. The crates sit next to each other on the tray with a rope around them as if the glass bottles aren't delicate at all. The pop colours are right, but not the taste. It doesn't stay in your mouth like the real thing and it doesn't get cold enough. If, say, you had a friend over after school and you poured it into a glass with some ice while they weren't looking, you could get away with the orange pop but not the cola. Coke is too special.

The driver of the truck doesn't wear a uniform but the door of the truck is painted red and the word *Pop* is written on it at an angle with bubbles coming off like you've just twisted the cap. Driving the pop truck would be a good job for a father to do.

At school I learnt that humans are descended from fish. There's nothing to say that evolution has stopped. Because of cars our legs might shrink and we could go back to being fish again. At school I learnt about sets. A set is a collection. First you identify a common property among things and then you gather up all the things that share this common property. In a collection of men not all of them are fathers. A set of fathers has the one thing in common, but it might not be obvious. (In a set of bachelors some of them could be secret fathers.) Once you've identified a set of fathers there are still many different types. The awkward father is best. There's the pitiful father, the angry father, the father that has been cut loose. There's the forgetful father, or the father that was so fine and so handsome and so happy that when the time before is over he can't go on, and he disappears.

Fathers can be made to do things. Most of the time it's driving from one place to another, but you can also make him lift things and go and get things. He will not be happy about it – he'd rather be with men – but he will do it anyway. When you are old enough a father will hire a suit and hold his arm out so you can grip on to it and you don't trip over in your big dress. Even if he never had you, a father will get to give you away.

There is less risk underneath the bed than on top of it. Dead flies under here, and tissues that have gone hard. I find the consolation prize certificate for grade five penmanship under my bed. The cardboard is creased now. A consolation prize is for comfort after a loss. The certificate says, *Have Pen – Can Write.* But where would I begin? What would I start to say?

^

My birthday. Here we are still breathing. Air particles are tiny. It must be some of the same air going into us all. We sit in a line at the table to eat. We sit in a line in front of the television to watch. The toilet is private but you know when someone has been there before you. A car leaves; a car comes back. Breakages are common under the blue sky. Only some of the broken things are ever fixed. The cicadas stitch their song into the day.

This day, during which we continue to breathe, is not a still life. A day is not a cloud study. It is not music (even good music you can nutbush to). It is not a limerick. A day is not three kisses scratched inside a birthday card. There is no card; there is no cake. There was once a vase on the table. It was from the time before. A fluted glass vase with bubbles caught inside. It never held flowers and then it broke. A day is just time. Sometimes, but rarely so, a bird will sing. There is nothing that this day can give you. It has nothing. The day doesn't know you were born on it years ago and it couldn't say happy birthday even if it did.

I am not that much in my bedroom on my birthday. I am in the kitchen, then I'm in the hallway. Later I'm in the workshop. Here is the engine cradle – you don't have to touch it – just to be near. Here is the test battery on its trolley. I am full of acid today. I am the snake in the woodpile that curls back on itself, poison dripping from its fangs.

Father man is out on the highway fixing a repair that has broken down again. I wonder if he will have to return the money and what excuses he'll make. I sit on the stool in front of the workbench and put Sharon's shell from the beach to my ear. There's no noise, but perhaps I need to give it time? The sea might be inside the shell, just trapped and having trouble getting its sound out.

At the end of our trip in the blue car we spent three days in the stranger's beds, on the stranger's toilet, on the stranger's chairs, before we drove home again. The shop near the stranger's house made sandwiches for our lunch at the beach. We had roast meat sandwiches with tomato sauce on white bread with margarine and salt and pepper. The girl put on plastic gloves to make the sandwiches. She had an electric carving knife that roared and worried at the roast meat until it fell into slices. Big animals eat smaller animals without any of the wrapping, or the extras. When a fox catches a rabbit does it eat the tastiest bits first or leave them for the last bite?

We took the meat sandwiches to the beach. It was hard with the flies, and with the tide out so far we were sitting at the edge of a giant puddle. My mother brought her handbag and the specials catalogue from Woolworths.

It turns out the specials are the same all over Australia. Father man stayed at the stranger's house because the cricket had to be listened to. There were other people on the beach with eskies and large coloured towels and music and balls and umbrellas. My mother put the Woolworths catalogue over her head to block out the sun and we lay on the hot sand. My brother said we were too old to make a sandcastle and he didn't want to bury me.

We didn't know what to do at the beach. We weren't qualified. There was no surf to jump in. There were no large shells to pick up and take home so you could hear it forever, just the small shell I put in my pocket for Sharon. The actual sea was silent. I'd heard it before on television, though. Hot Lips on *Mash* has a dream that she's walking along a beach with Major Frank Burns. Hot Lips is wearing a bikini and the wind from the sea is frothing her white hair all around her head. The dry sound of romantic music was mixed up with the wet sound of the waves, so it wasn't easy even then to unpick the sound of the sea and hear it just on its own.

I put Sharon's shell on the workbench and tap it, gently. Not much force is needed when using father man's hammer.

The next day there's a moth trapped in my room. The moth flies against the window. Sometimes it lands on the curtains for a rest. Wings open, wings closed, wings a-tremble. My mother is at work. My brother is at cricket. There isn't much time in between the beat of a moth's wings, but this afternoon it is enough.

Afterwards there's the rag that has fallen from father man's pocket. I hide it in my schoolbag. Perhaps I could wrap it up later and give it as a gift – a filthy scarf for my mother?

The Valiant is out. Darren's spare door key hangs from a string in his meter box. His house has green carpet covered with plastic mats in the hallways and on all the major routes. Every house has its own bad smell. Darren's collection of matches is on the bookcase next to the television. Matchbooks and matchboxes. There are old ones from history and ones from other countries. On top of the television is a glass jar full of thin matchbooks from pubs. Barmaids put the matchbooks in the ashtrays and anyone can take them, so Darren wasn't stealing. Darren has a giant matchstick with a blue tip mounted on hooks above the television. The giant match says *Disneyland USA* in gold lettering on the pale wood of the stick; its red head is rough and spackled. Not easy to strike such a heavy match. I scrape it over the concrete trough in the laundry. I scrape it again and again.

'God bless Mickey Mouse,' I say, as the match hisses

into flame. I march backwards and forwards on Darren's green carpet, holding big Disney in front of me as she burns.

There's a letter in the letterbox from school that says I've missed more than the acceptable number of days. My attendance is irregular and the school must be informed of any illness. I put the letter in the fat lady's letterbox. First I scratch out my name. Then I write in hers.

Nobody is concerned about the television that we missed when we were away. Some of the shows seem to have a story but it turns out you can take a break from them and there's nothing you don't know. I like how females look on television. They decorate their hair with a scarf or a ribbon and their ears with a jewel or a bead pushed through a hole in the earlobe. There are charm bracelets with dangling love hearts and puppy dogs and telephones for the girls with good skin that don't have any trouble with time. One minute the girls are cute six; next they are sweet sixteen. The girls and the women know to let the laughing go up and down and then fade out before they speak, and they know always to wait for the men and the boys to get their speaking done first.

She should be cautious, but a girl should not be silent. She should have a voice that tinkles like a bell. Words are made in the head and sent down to the throat for speaking. It happens instantly. Except when a part is broken and the words go around and around inside instead. If they ever found their way out who knows what mess they would make?

The lady on the back seat of the bus pulls the cord for the next stop. The bus corners. An inner wheel rotates on a smaller radius than the outer wheel when the vehicle describes a curve. The lady's bra strap slides over the meat of her shoulder and tap, tap, taps against her elbow. Low gear for the slow descent. Warning signs for the truck arrester bed. A telephone in a blue box to call for the crane. The lady with the fallen bra strap has dropped her bus ticket. She's making her way to the front door. Maybe she won't need it, but I lean down and pick the ticket up off the floor near the wheel arch.

'Here,' I call out to her. 'You dropped this.'

Sixty days, then, without words. To speak you have to learn not to listen to yourself. You have to trust what might come out of you into the plain day air.

Shaft. Sphere. Yoke. Spring. Rod. Engine speech is clean.

The workshop holds the brown night in the way a pool holds water. The darkness weakens at the walls where the jam jars and tobacco tins and rags wait on the metal shelves.

The shadow board glows above the workbench, each tool held snug inside its painted outline. A tool doesn't like to be the only tool taken. Don't stint. Take all the tools you'll need for the job at hand. A mirror hangs from a nail above the bench. A small mirror is useful in the workshop for checking oil leaks, for seeing the underside of a part. Substance and reflection. Surprising how much light the mirror soaks up from the darkness. A shock to see what has become of my face as it goes about its crime.

When you go out at night to hurt the fat lady's Mini you have to take a lot for granted. You have to believe that the black night air can be breathed like the clear day air. You have to trust the ground will take your weight even though you can't see your feet as they press down upon it. You don't have to worry about the darkness. The stars always make enough light to identify the parts to be hurt. It's never too much. Once a bonnet is open the stars draw closer. The shiny engine beams up at the stars; the shiny stars beam down at the engine. Perhaps it is beautiful that my hands can bring them together?

Time to take the Mini out on the highway now. The fat lady has cut two patterned Axminster carpet squares from the rug in her dining room as car mats so it's like driving a room of her house, which is a comfort for me.

I park the Mini near the arrester bed and sit and watch for a while just in case it's the night for a brake failure, and for one of the big trucks to ditch.

I would like to see the face of the man in the cab as he ditches. I'd like to see his attitude as he steers and stamps and steers and stamps on the slack brake. I would like to see the weight of the trailers catching up behind him, coming down around his shoulders like an avalanche that he's so busy running from he can't see it coming.

On the way back the Mini stalls on the incline of the driveway. I have to do a hill start close to the side of the house where my mother and father man are sleeping in their bed. No matter about the noise. I am invisible tonight.

An engine can tolerate a small amount of disturbance – sand, for instance – but gradually, over time, the effect of the disturbance increases. A handful of sand – a female-sized handful – might be within working limits, but after that just one more grain is enough to tip the operation into seizure.

My mother puts the radio on every evening when she's getting ready for bed. If you listen to the top ten you could think that someone's coming to get you. If you stay still, if you stay in one place, and play the same song over and over, sooner or later a boy will come with a guitar and pointed fingernails and the plastic lozenge he uses to pluck the strings. The music will be all around you and he'll look at your hair as he sings.

Nobody is coming to get me, which is good because I wouldn't have the right jeans if they did.

I heard father man sing a song once. We were on our trip. We were having lunch at a roadhouse on the plains. The sausage rolls were hard to swallow, too much dry material banking up in the mouth. There was an old white cocky in a cage on top of the gas bottles outside. 'Dance-cocky-dance,' father man sang at it. Then he took my mother's hand and said, 'put your finger in there.'

More rain today. The rain touches gently. It isn't vicious. It wets everyone just the same. I like to walk in the rain. Down Struttle Road hill, just past the bus stop, just under the street lamp, the smell of burning rubber is sweet on the wet air. The fat lady's green Mini is crumpled in the roadside ditch. The driver's door is open. I don't go to it, because not far ahead a swollen tree has fallen across the road. Not all of it is across the road; its legs and the hem of its dress are on the gravel in between the road and the bush. The road is taut but the fat lady is slack upon it, the pieces of her heaped up like rubbish. I lean over and look at the wet strings of her yellow hair where they are fixed to her pink head. I look at the water in the bowl of her ear and down the front of her dress where one white tit is pleated up against the other. Her fat eyes are closed and airy bubbles are foaming from her mouth.

The fat lady likes to ride the clutch. I always knew when she'd gone out driving from the papery smell of the clutch face burning, like someone trying to light a whole wet newspaper at once. Her Mini has a two brush, two pole, shunt wound generator unit controlled by a generator regulator. It was easy enough for two small hands to slacken the pivot bolts and brace nut and push the generator towards the engine. I prised the fuse cover off the fuse board too. All the tiny circuits like a field of flowers, like the weeds on the fat lady's dress.

I like the sound my raincoat makes as I walk around the fat lady on the road. Nobody else can hear the plastic as it rustles, but it sounds loud and good to me. I think the fat lady has been here since before it started raining because the road underneath her is pale and dry. I think she staggered from the crashed car and then she fell. There are old tissues in my pocket that I use for the blood. The lady that sells duck eggs further up the hill makes the phone calls and I don't have to wait because I am a girl and I need to be getting home. People seem to think it isn't safe for a girl to be out in the rain.

^

The next evening my mother went to her dancing class and my brother was watching television. The window above the television and the window in my bedroom are on the same side of the house. They look out to the same place.

It didn't take long. Not much longer than an ad break.

My brother wouldn't have seen this because he can't look away from the television screen, but when I turned my head to the side and looked out of the window the hopping bird was back again. Its withered claw a tangle of roots sprouting from its scruffy body. The hopping bird jerked across the verandah, throwing itself forwards, leading with its beak. There are steps but the hopping bird didn't take the smooth surface; instead it tilted into the garden bed and hopped and fell and hopped and fell across the dirt and stones.

Father man shuddered and then he winced. On the other side of the wall the ads for toys were over and it was back to the show.

Once a crime is made on you there's a stickiness, as if the crime is bait to draw other crimes near. When you think about what happened to you it can be confusing because other crimes are there, or around about, in the same place. Some of the crimes are part of your story; others are part of the stories of other people that you might be taking as your own.

The only way to tell what really belongs to a person would be if a film was made of your life – if a camera hung over you every minute of every day and every night. If you had this film you could press the button to make it play backwards and there you would be: un-putting your clothes on, un-brushing your hair, getting down from bed, waiting to be un-touched.

If everyone had their personal film, who would own the parts of the film where a family comes together? When families are assembled for talking, eating, watching television; when families are driving in cars and sitting on buses and passing each other on the street; and then, later, coming together in fear and in despair?

That night, I pack a bag and run away to the tip. I'm not really living anywhere. There's nowhere to sleep, mainly I'm walking but because I come back in the morning to feed the baby skinks nobody knows that I was gone.

The next evening, as soon as it gets dark, I walk back up Davidsons Road towards the tip again. I don't know if I'll stay over. It's been a hot day, again. Cicadas are drumming in their family band. The warm road bakes the bottom of my sandals. It might be time for a kangaroo. The chugging is Darren's white Valiant coming up behind me. It's a V8. Valiant means manful; it means brave. Smooth through the synchromesh into second, a squeeze of brake. The engine rumbles; the muffler grunts. It's hard for a car to keep time with a girl walking when the car is hot and petrol-rich. Perhaps Darren is wearing his shire raincoat? He wouldn't have known I'd be out walking now, but here I am. He has his high beams on. The headlights paint my hair, my shoulders, my bum, the backs of my legs. I swerve a little towards the bush. One sandal slaps the gravel in front of the other. The looseness of the sandals around my feet will slow me down when I need to run.

The Valiant keeps an even distance, then Darren cuts the headlights and the road rears up blackly in front of me. Can he see me? When is the right time to run? The air is going in and then going out of me hot and jerky. The air is catching on something where my throat is narrow – perhaps it is a word?

But listen, another engine is approaching, another car is coming up behind the Valiant. Darren is blocking the road now; there could be an accident. He has no choice but to flip his lights back on and accelerate ahead. The weight and the wind of the long white car as it passes, the feel of it across my cheek. He drives away; he cuts me free.

Warm piss between my thighs. I am running. I don't run into the bush; I run across the road, down a driveway, into a double carport. I crouch between a warm Volvo and a cold Gemini – one hand on the door panel of each.

The cars belong to a house I went to once. I know I won't ever go there again.

Last winter the girl of this house was cleaning her horse trough in the paddock by the road. She saw me walking past and called out and said I could help her. We dragged the green weed that grows on the inside walls of the concrete trough out with our hands. The water was so cold it hurt, then we went inside to use the soap. The mother was in the kitchen in her slippers. The girl said, 'Mum, where's the vanilla slice?' There were baking things out on the counter and on the windowsill there were dolls-of-the-world on their stands. The Spanish doll is the one you'd want to be with her red lace dress and her wad of black hair. The vanilla slice was cooling in the fridge so we couldn't have it for five minutes. Then the mum gave us both a plate, a paper serviette and a glass of Milo. You could see where the knife had dragged through the icing but apart from that it was the same vanilla slice that you buy at the shop. I felt sick in my throat from the custard. They had a rug in the toilet. They had a toilet brush with a doll's head and a skirt around it. The girl's mum was fat. The mum watched us as we ate. I think she was trying to make us fat like her.

That time, there was only the Gemini in the carport with an empty space next to it, because the father was at work. Now it is night-time and the Volvo is home too.

Here I am doing something nice for myself. There's a bath in the bathroom but nobody ever uses it so you have to wipe the broken hair out of it first and pick a time when everyone is out. At the start of the bath you take off your t-shirt and jeans and underpants and put them on the top of the toilet with the lid closed. In the mirror above the sink the bra has left red lines on your shoulders and under your arms. Out of the harness now and into the water. There's dishwashing liquid for bubbles. Use as much as you think they won't notice is gone. The bubbles are cheerful and full of colours. They stick to the parts of you that are out of the water in the same way they stick to the cups and the bowls and the plates in the sink.

Under the surface both of my ears swallow water. When I come up and reach for the towel a sound comes out that could have been laughing. Yes, it sounded like a girl laughing. If I'd had a knife I would have cut that sound out. It was a clean sound and you could have cut it neatly, without leaving any ragged edges behind.

When my brother gets home from school he can do eight slices of toast and I can do five. Once you take the loaf out of the plastic bag you can't predict where it will separate and fall apart. In America they have thin bread for sandwiches and thick bread for toast. The *Brady Bunch* maid can't make up her mind which one to buy as the girls like it one way and the boys like it the other. I can't see thin bread ever taking off here.

My brother puts a butterknife in the toaster when the bread gets stuck and he never bothers to unplug it first. A problem for girls is you are often afraid and it always shows on your face. The time my brother threw kerosene into the firebox of the boiler because it wouldn't light, the fire woofed back at him as happy as a pup. What were those black ticks falling from him? His eyebrows turning to twigs.

The problem of my brother is that he must be left behind. He can't drive yet. He has to have the television. He has to have a ball. The gap between boy and man is always bigger than between girl and woman. If there's gravel in the hub cap my brother wouldn't empty it; he'd cover his ears. Men have places inside themselves where they can put things. I hope for my brother it comes in soon.

Vitas Gerulaitis is on television. Vitas Gerulaitis with his big curly perm bouncing on his shoulders. He does a funny dance with his tennis racquet and everyone laughs. Then it's the news. Some Aboriginal boys are living in wrecks in the desert. The wrecks have different-coloured door panels and some have been burnt and some have been painted with leftover house paint so the boys look like they're living under big, happy patchwork quilts, except that they are broken-down cars.

When a part is damaged all of the surrounding parts are put at risk. The site of the fresh damage can be far removed, in time and in place, from the cause.

The fat lady has knitted me a cardigan in hospital and now she's home I have to go over and get it. It is a white cardigan with pink stitching on the collar. The size of the cardigan is tiny. It is for a small girl – a toddler, even. There are rows and rows of lumpy stitches so it doesn't sit flat when I take it out of the tissue paper and lay it on the fat lady's kitchen table. The cardigan looks like someone's body is already inside it. I hold the cardigan up in front of my chest. The fat lady says sorry, when it should have been me.

Last summer, before the trip in the Holden, I thought the cicadas sang only for me. Most days I parted the wires of the fence and walked up to the bush behind the house. It isn't a sanctuary. It's just scrub. The gum trees are all burnt. Some have fallen over. The bark of the trees is covered in charcoal that stains and doesn't come off in the wash, so it's a pity, but you can't sit on them. There's lots of holly banksia with every one of its needle leaves waiting to prick you. There might have been a kangaroo on its way to and from the tip. On the days that I saw a kangaroo I would tell myself the world was clean.

This summer, now that we are back, I know that the kangaroo will never stop and look at me. Calling it on a gumleaf is no use at all; it won't come like Skippy. A kangaroo can't be bothered with someone like me. It will keep on bouncing as if I haven't been born, or as if I am already dead.

Another good thing about our trip on the road was that all of the bits of me were in one place for a while, on the back seat of the car. Now they are coming apart again. You don't know how good a holiday can be until you get home. The other good thing about our trip, about being on the road that I miss, is that none of the people who were also on the road knew who we were, so nobody bothered to turn away.

I buy a headlight globe for the Holden from the tyre boy at the automotive. I don't have any need of it. It's three dollars and seventy-five cents. I give him a five-dollar note. The boy is chewing gum and it isn't a new piece. I can see, when he opens his mouth to say the price of the globe, the hard white turd of the gum tumbling around in his mouth.

Buying the globe was a challenge I set for myself, a test. If I was someone else the tyre boy would have smiled and bought me a can of Fanta and told me that I could be his and that he would look after me forever and a day. The tyre boy hands me the change and I put it in my schoolbag with the globe. Neither of us speaks. It doesn't matter. The boy is all the parts of his story. It wouldn't be possible for him to say them to me as he stands behind the counter at the automotive, and if he did I would never be able to say mine in return.

Walking home I notice a lucerne tree is upset by the wind but only one piece of it – the rest of the tree is too tired to shake its leaves around. I'd like to say the tree was waving at me, but it wouldn't be true. Sometimes you see a woman with a man's hands. That's not so bad. When you see a man with a woman's hands it's best to look away. Any sort of machine can be a place to put your mind, but one with an engine is best.

It's a long walk home along the side of the highway, and because of the globe and the boy in the automotive I know now what has been taken from me. It's confusing, this exchange, because sometimes you could think, with what's left behind, that you are being given something. But no, it's a taking. Father man has taken my chance to tell all of the parts of my story. There will always be this part that can never be told.

I don't go up to the workshop when I get home. I get the penknife out from under my bed. I stole one for Sharon

185

from the camping store and I stole one for me. I unwrap the penknife from its rag and test how it does its cutting.

A Monday/Tuesday dream: I am driving a cage down the highway. The sun paints the bitumen with leaf light. The cage is tall and airy and clean. Its wire is made from tennis racquet strings. The view is good although a little crisscrossed. No door to be found. No escape.

A Friday/Saturday dream: I am driving across the purple sea. My brother is in his bed on the back seat of the sea car. His lumps are in the right places under the blanket. All good. All sealed. No water is getting in.

A Sunday dream: I am riding down the highway on a pony. There's a lot of traffic. The road is thick with horses and ponies in both directions. Someone hollers at me as they pass. Cortina girl is in the next lane. Her silver spurs glint in the sun as she trots past.

'Come with me,' she calls over her shoulder. 'Come on!' Each horse and pony has its engine capacity painted across its rump. Horsepower is a unit to measure the rate at which work is done. It's a happy dream. It's fun to be in among them all.

A throaty bird in the tall pines this morning. The roller door is open. I have never seen my mother in the workshop, but here's her red and white headscarf balled up on father man's stool. The scarf goes over my mother's head and ties behind her ears. It's colourful and on the weekends it takes the place of her hair. I don't like to see it here. I don't want it spoiled by the tools and parts.

There are thoughts inside my head that require the death of everyone in the world, except me. I don't need violence. I don't need blood or corpses. I just need to be on my own but with fully stocked shops, and hopefully with TV.

Do I take the manual? Can I just take the hands? There could be different views. *Exploded View of Stroking of the Skin. Exploded View of Tickling. Exploded View of a Pair of Feet That Want to Dance.* The dancing feet don't worry about how they might look in the picture. The music throb, throb, throbs in their ankles just for fun.

A last walk to the tip to say goodbye to the kangaroos. Not much rubbish around, the bulldozers have been in to bury it. No sign of Darren's Valiant. It won't be going anywhere for a while.

A last episode of *Mash* with my brother.

A last drive with my mother. We are out to buy milk in the dark. My mother has forgotten to put the headlights of the Holden on. A truck coming in the opposite direction toots its air horn at us. My mother cringes and makes a sour mouth. She applies more of her foot to the accelerator, but she doesn't turn the headlights on.

A last feed of flies for the skinks.

A last lap around the garden to farewell the buried kittens, to farewell the buried parts.

The fall of night, the break of day. All the metal on the hills, all the metal in the road. Too much is broken now. Time to leave.

It's dawn. The house is quiet. No big claims here. Just the usual. Except I take the keys from father man's pocket, unlock the deadlock and leave the house through the door. I walk across the brown lawn, under the pine trees, to the workshop and roll up the roller door. I release the tools from the shadow board. As they fall to the floor, I say their names aloud: wrench, ratchet, saw, hammer, grips... My voice is a little rusty, but strong enough on top of the new day air. My feet are in my sneakers. I am wearing all of my best clothes. Hardly any choke is needed to start father man's Holden, to drive it down the ramp, down the driveway, to press it through the glinting morning light.

My hands are steady on the steering wheel. Just a

little numbness in my chest. I remember our trip, when we were all driving together. If I look over my shoulder I expect I might see myself on the back seat. We were always coming into places and going out of places; we were always on the road. One day we crossed seven rivers together, but none of them had water. Steep descent, steep climb, narrow bridge, divided road, loose surface, crest, lane closed, stop. The road words are stored inside me now. I will keep them safe.

I turn onto the highway. Up through the gears, gain some speed. It isn't possible to drive in reverse for any great distance. Too much distortion. You wouldn't get far – you would never reach the time before. A dawn rabbit in the roadside weeds decides to cross ahead of me. The rabbit leaps in front of the rolling tyres and, just making it, jumps at the bank on the other side of the road, but the bank is a wall of broken gravel – leavings from roadworks now forgotten. The rabbit's feet contact the gravel but fail to grip. It falls backwards through the bright air towards the road again. The rabbit falls sweetly, without hurry, its ears long and heavy behind it in the way a child's hair clumps, damp from the bath. On the road now, a sack of startled rabbit meat cracks to juice beneath my tyre. It's something to feel sad about – the other rabbits huddled in the burrow, waiting for its return.

∧

What is left? Transmission and exchange, the coming together of the mating faces of the parts. If you use the windscreen for your eyes, the films of the mind can be prevented from playing.

Your choice – keep driving forever through the day and night, or, if you want it to end, to be held, you can use the arrester bed.

No one is about to see me so early in the morning, hurtling down the hill. I wind the window down. Goodbye to Sharon's bus stop, to the petrol station with the automotive next door; goodbye to the new Olympic swimming pool, to the parked trailer waiting to be sold. Increasing speed, decreasing time. The warning signs have their faces turned towards the sun. Round the corner. A test for the tyres, to hold the curve at speed. The cage of gravel in front of me. Do I indicate? Too late.

The gravel takes the steering wheel from my hands, snapping the tyres from left to right. The impact isn't sudden; it isn't hitting. Two elements are meeting in an exchange of motion, in a transfer of danger. Windedness. Grogginess. Thick orange dust, like smoke, like panic, rising. The gravel has control now. The body of gravel is rising fast, sucking motion into stillness. The gravel forces its way into the engine, into all of the spaces between the parts. It obliterates the exploded view. The gravel seeps into the car now. It pushes against me – it pushes against all the bits of me equally, as if my arm, my back, my elbow, my foot are no different to my breasts and to my sex. The gravel presses into me and some of its pieces are sharp against my neck.

Quiet here now. The dust settling a little, air enough to breathe. I am the one that reared up. I am the one that got away. Very soon now, just a few minutes, before I shrug off these stones. When it happens it will be fast, so fast it will be impossible to measure.

All the valves inside me are releasing. I use both feet to force the door of the Holden open. I fold onto the gravel, and away.